"Thanks for evening, Mr. Rees."

"Such polite, well-bred sentiments, Mrs. Barton." Dai gently caressed Gina's cheek. "Have you really enjoyed yourself?"

"I really have," Gina answered nervously. Dai's touch was sending shivers through her whole body. "The meal was excellent, and the restaurant—"

"Then your 'lovely evening' had nothing to do with you and me?" Dai cut in, his eyes gleaming wickedly. "Don't kid yourself, Gina. We're an explosion just waiting to happen. You've got a lot of catching up to do—and I'm the man you're going to do it with."

Gina drew in her breath sharply. "And just what makes you so sure of yourself?" she demanded.

"It's what makes the world go round" was Dai's almost matter-of-fact response. "And you're not going to miss out on your share of it, any more than I am."

Rowan Kirby, happily married for eighteen years to an ex-research scientist, has two teenage children and lives near Bristol. With a degree in English, she has spent time teaching English to foreign students and has been involved in adult literacy. She always wanted to write, and has had articles published both in newspapers and in women's magazines. To date, four of her romance novels have been accepted by Harlequin. Her aim, she says, is to inject some new realism into the genre.

Books by Rowan Kirby

Don't miss any of our special offers. Write to us at the following address for information on our newest releases.

Harlequin Reader Service
901 Fuhrmann Blvd., P.O. Box 1397, Buffalo, NY 14240
Canadian address: P.O. Box 603,
Fort Erie, Ont. L2A 5X3

Fusion
Rowan Kirby

Harlequin Books

TORONTO • NEW YORK • LONDON
AMSTERDAM • PARIS • SYDNEY • HAMBURG
STOCKHOLM • ATHENS • TOKYO • MILAN

Original hardcover edition published in 1985
by Mills & Boon Limited

ISBN 0-373- 02847-4

Harlequin Romance first edition July 1987

For Martin
(for everything)

Copyright © 1985 by Rowan Kirby.
Philippine copyright 1985. Australian copyright 1985.
All rights reserved. Except for use in any review, the reproduction or utilization
of this work in whole or in part in any form by any electronic, mechanical
or other means, now known or hereafter invented, including xerography,
photocopying and recording, or in any information storage or retrieval system,
is forbidden without the permission of the publisher, Harlequin Enterprises
Limited, 225 Duncan Mill Road, Don Mills, Ontario, Canada M3B 3K9. All the
characters in this book have no existence outside the imagination of the
author and have no relation whatsoever to anyone bearing the same name
or names. They are not even distantly inspired by any individual known
or unknown to the author, and all incidents are pure invention.

The Harlequin trademarks, consisting of the words HARLEQUIN ROMANCE
and the portrayal of a Harlequin, are trademarks of Harlequin Enterprises
Limited; the portrayal of a Harlequin is registered in the United States Patent
and Trademark Office and in the Canada Trade Marks Office.

Printed in U.S.A.

CHAPTER ONE

ANOTHER sultry, stuffy afternoon dragged to its close. Gina Barton, busy at her desk, wondered why it was that London never seemed to be ready for extremes of temperature. Sweltering summers, arctic winters—residents of the great city were infallibly outraged by either.

Pity, she thought, gazing out of her window, that the firm didn't run to air conditioning. Still, at least it was relatively cool and calm in the office. Things could be a lot worse: she could be out there among the July sales, shouldering her way through steaming, exhausted, thirsty crowds. She shuddered at such a prospect of hell on earth; a nightmare.

Not far away, in the West End, another woman had spent her day doing exactly that. For Mrs Peggy Haines, however, the nightmare was only beginning. At that precise moment—as she stood wearily outside the department store she had just left, loaded with parcels—she was being arrested for shoplifting. Neither Gina nor Peggy was aware of it yet, but that moment was destined to link and change their lives.

It was no less mercilessly hot two days later, when Peggy and her husband Jim—a stock-supervisor in a warehouse—arrived at the shop-fronted premises of Messrs Goldman and Gillow, Solicitors and Commissioners for Oaths. They waited for a few minutes in an airy outer lobby, liberally strewn with magazines (which Peggy was far too nervous to read) and brightened with cut flowers. Then they were shown into a smaller inner office.

'Mr and Mrs Haines,' explained the friendly

secretary, flashing them a reassuring grin as she ushered them through the door.

'Thank you, Michele.' The voice was warm, pleasantly low—and very female. The person now waiting for them behind a well-organised desk matched it perfectly. She looked up as they came in; and the slight frown which had furrowed her high, smooth brow as she studied some notes disappeared into a totally sweet, natural smile, reaching right to the depths of her shining dark eyes.

'Good morning, Mrs Haines—Mr Haines. Won't you sit down?'

Peggy perched on the edge of one of the two chairs drawn up at the desk, clutching her handbag tensely against her. She stared at the young woman opposite. She had hardly known what to expect, but it certainly hadn't been someone like this. She found herself looking into a round intelligent face, with well-defined cheekbones, a small pointed chin, a slightly turned-up nose, a wide generous mouth—and those remarkable eyes, which were a most unusual shade of . . . what was it? Peggy deliberated . . . almost a sort of golden-brown. Yes, that was it—a lovely warm hazel, flecked with gold.

The creamy olive complexion was flawless; the hair richly dark—again, thought Peggy, you couldn't just call it brown. It was a deep glossy chestnut, long and straight, falling from a centre parting to frame her face, and wound now into a thick coil at her nape, neat and efficient.

Her whole bearing was neat and efficient, but strikingly feminine. Only her top half was visible, of course, behind the desk; but you could see enough of that to know the young woman was decidedly well-rounded—her soft curves certainly not disguised by her dove-grey silk blouse, its short sleeves revealing plump tanned arms as satin-smooth as the material itself. Two delicate gold bracelets encircled one trim wrist; and there was a single gold band, Peggy noticed (as women usually do notice) on the ring finger of her left hand.

Jim Haines cleared his throat. Despite her tension, his wife almost smiled. Jim was never immune to the charms of a young lady—especially one as charming as this. 'Morning, Miss,' he returned her polite greeting as he took a seat.

The heartwarming smile appeared again as she became aware of them both studying her. 'What can we do for you?' She glanced at her notes. 'Ah yes—you 'phoned, didn't you?' It seemed to Peggy that she exuded an air of tranquillity. The atmosphere round her was like a peaceful oasis in a frantic world. She began to relax, just a little, under its influence.

'Are you—er—Goldman or Gillow?' Jim was enquiring bluntly. Peggy frowned at him in mute reproof; but the young woman simply laughed, showing small white teeth, her eyes sharing in the amusement.

'Neither. I'm their junior partner. My name's Gina Barton. How d'you do?'

She stood up and walked around the desk to shake them by the hand, each in turn. She was of medium height, and the grey blouse was tucked neatly into the waistband of a wide black skirt in crisp cotton, falling over rounded hips. Without looking at him, Peggy knew that Jim would be appreciating those shapely bare brown calves, tapering to slim ankles and plain grey leather wedge-heeled sandals.

'Pleased to meet you, Miss Barton.' Jim, who had also risen, now sat down again.

'How do you do, *Mrs* Barton,' added Peggy pointedly.

'Now,' Gina Barton invited in her low, sweet tones, 'how about telling me all about it? I gather you've been the victim of a . . . misunderstanding? Accused of shoplifting—is that right, Mrs Haines?'

'That's right,' confirmed Jim. 'A misunderstanding. She was . . .'

The gentle smile turned full on to him; the softly spoken interruption concealed an unmistakable command. 'Shall we let your wife speak for herself, Mr Haines? I always like to hear a story straight from the horse's mouth—if you'll pardon the expression.' There was nothing strident in the suggestion—merely the most low-key of requests.

Jim subsided, glancing at his wife. 'Sure, of course,' he muttered. He had only been trying to protect her—something he was used to doing from way, way back.

'Now then, Mrs Haines.' Her expression indicated that she was all ears.

'Well, it was like this,' Peggy faltered, returning Jim's glance. 'I was shopping in Oxford Street. I'd been there all day and I'd nearly finished . . .' It was painful at first, reconstructing the events of that dreadful afternoon. The rigidly impassive face of the store detective; the interview with the harassed manager; the arrival of the brash young police officer who had warned her that 'anything she said might be taken down and used in evidence', just like in plays on television; the ride in the Black Maria; the undignified 'processing' at the police station—fingerprints, photographs, statements, handbag and body searches . . .

But Gina Barton made it as easy as she could—listening intently to every syllable, prompting here, asking a pertinent question there—always keeping up, even a step ahead. When Peggy reached the most difficult bits she nodded sympathetically, pursing up her curved lips.

'. . . I'd collected some underwear for Jim and Gary. Then I saw this little vest—pink, it was, with lace round the neck. Julie loves pretty clothes, but it was quite expensive so I thought about it a bit. Then I decided to have it, so I put it with the other things. Or I thought I did.' Her voice trembled. 'I walked to the checkout and paid. I was ever so tired, Mrs Barton. It was such a hot day. I showed them the ticket but all they kept saying was, even though I'd paid for everything else, I'd stolen the vest. It was horrible. They wouldn't believe me, whatever I said . . .'

She scrabbled for a handkerchief, and Gina leaned over the desk, her eyes now brimming with kindly concern. 'Take your time, Mrs Haines. There's no rush.'

At last it was all out. Peggy sat back in her chair, a new relief surging through her. Gina put both elbows on the desk top and linked her small fingers together under her chin as she gazed across at them both. 'I see,' she said slowly. 'So—you pleaded Not Guilty before the Magistrates yesterday, and your case comes up again in about a month?'

'That's right,' Peggy agreed miserably.

Jim, who had held his peace dutifully throughout his wife's long tale, couldn't restrain an anxious interruption. 'She did the right thing, didn't she, not to plead Guilty? They tried to tell her she should—said she'd never get away with it. But I told her she should only say she was guilty if she knew she was.'

'You were absolutely right, Mr Haines.' The dark head nodded vehemently. 'You should do as your conscience dictates. If you feel innocent, then *on no account*'—she emphasised these last three words in her careful, modulated tone—'should you allow yourself to be persuaded otherwise. Remember, you're innocent until the law proves you guilty. Even if it takes far longer, you must fight for what *you* know to be the truth. It's a good thing you were there to advise her,' she added with a wide smile.

'That's what I told her.' Jim basked in the light from Gina Barton's approval. She had a way of approving, though she was barely aware of it herself, which could make strong men glow in its reflection.

'A conviction for shoplifting,' she went on now, 'is a conviction under the Theft Act. If you are found Guilty of this, you will have a record for theft, as surely as if you'd broken into a house and stolen private property. There are some people who think that's unfair, and it ought to be changed—but at the moment, that's how it is.' She shrugged. 'One day perhaps it'll be different.'

'But plenty of real thieves must steal from shops,' Peggy suggested hesitantly. 'I mean—like, on purpose. I suppose they have to be ... I mean ... punished?'

'Sure they do. And they are; the law deals with them firmly, when they're caught. No one's denying they deserve all they get.'

'*When* they're caught,' echoed Jim, with a touch of cynicism.

'Oh, they often are,' Gina assured him. 'All the same, it's people like you I'm sorry for, Mrs Haines— caught in the trap. Everyone knows how easy it is to slip up in these big shops, especially at busy times. I've come near enough doing it myself; who hasn't?'

Peggy was warming to this direct young woman more every minute. It seemed to her they had struck lucky when they selected this firm of solicitors, almost at random, from the local Yellow Pages. 'I just couldn't believe what was going on.' Her confidence restored itself, under the influence of those shining eyes. 'It didn't seem to be really happening—not to me, if you know what I mean. The vest was there, I admit, in my bag, but I never ... I mean, I never would ...'

'She never would,' Jim endorsed firmly. 'She may have her off-days, Miss ... Mrs Barton—don't we all have our absent-minded moments? But she'd never steal nothing from no one. I know my Peg.'

He was treated to the full impact of the melting smile for this loyal testimonial. Then Gina became brisk. 'Well—now that I've got all the details, we must take action. Of course we shall represent you. You've come to the right place—my senior partners and I are most concerned about such cases. We have more of them passing through our hands every month. We'll do all we can—but I have to warn you, it's not easy, convincing the Court that you've made a genuine error. I'm afraid they're getting harder and harder—not giving many people the benefit of the doubt.'

Peggy's face fell. 'You mean, I probably won't get off?'

'I didn't say that, Mrs Haines. There's—shall we say—a fifty/fifty chance? But we'll do absolutely everything we can. Would you like to be represented by Counsel?'

They looked at each other. 'Counsel?' echoed Jim, attempting not to sound baffled.

'A barrister,' Gina explained. 'There's all the more chance of getting off—of having your case put forward in the best possible way—if it's presented by an advocate who's trained to speak for people in Court.'

'Would I have to speak for myself, otherwise?' Peggy was aghast at the prospect.

'Good heavens, no. I can represent you myself, at a Magistrates' Court.'

'Does it cost much more?' Jim was not one to beat about the bush.

'Yes,' replied Gina honestly. 'But you might qualify for Legal Aid if it's difficult. We'll fill in all the forms in a minute. Now—what do you think?'

Her clients exchanged another glance. 'Do you have a . . . Counsel to recommend?' Jim enquired cautiously.

'Certainly—we work closely with several barristers. There's one who's particularly interested in this sort of case—he's taken quite a few for us.'

Peggy turned to Jim. 'Why not? We might as well have the best . . .'

He nodded. 'Okay. Ask him. Please,' he added quickly, catching Gina's eye.

She smiled. 'I'll give John Slade a ring as soon as I can,' she promised. 'Fix up a briefing with him.'

'Whatever you think best.' Peggy felt suddenly bemused by it all again.

'Briefing?' cut in Jim sharply.

'As a solicitor, I have to "brief" Counsel who is to

appear for you; that's my job. It just means telling them all about the case—preparing the ground so that they can go about it in the most constructive way. Once they have all the facts from me, it's up to them to use their persuasive powers, and our combined knowledge of the Law, to act on your behalf at the hearing. That's their job.' She grinned disarmingly. 'It's supposed to be teamwork, but sometimes I think we get landed with the donkeywork while they get the honour and glory. Still, I wouldn't want to be a barrister so I suppose I shouldn't complain. It's a very dramatic trade—winning's a personal achievement, but losing must be even worse than it is for us.'

'Well—if you say he's a good man . . .' began Jim.

'He is; and so are all his partners in Chambers—sharing his offices. Any of them would rise to a challenge like yours; I only hope one of them can take it on at rather short notice. I'll get on to them straight away. First, let's write down some of these boring details.' She opened out a daunting set of lengthy forms, took up a pen and embarked on filling the first one in. 'Full name?'

Two hours later, Gina walked across the central lobby and knocked on the door of another inner office.

'Come!' called a preoccupied voice from within. 'Ah, Gina,' it went on as she obeyed the succinct instruction. 'Lunchtime already? Come to invite me to lunch?' Button eyes twinkled at her from behind a mountain of paperwork.

'No, Sam. I'm quite sure you'll be wining and dining some high-powered client. You won't want me cluttering up the place.'

Sam Goldman—rotund, dumpy, bursting with energy and enthusiasm—was an excellent solicitor, well-known in the community for his liberal views, his championship of underdogs, and his willingness to take on difficult cases. A devoted family man himself, he inspired devotion in his staff—including Gina. 'You, my dear Gina,' he told her now, 'could never "clutter up" any place. However, now you mention it, I did say I'd meet old whatsisname—Renshaw, the Chamber of Commerce fellow—at the Bistro today. One or two small matters to discuss. Anything I can do for you before I go?'

'Yes, there is. Another Oxford Street shoplifting case arrived this morning. An unfortunate woman picked up a garment and walked out with it in her own shopping bag.'

He drew in a sharp breath. 'Sounds dodgy. Any mitigating circumstances?'

'Well, she did pay for a whole basketful of other clothes, all above-board. This one item—not particularly expensive—seems to have ended up in the wrong container—the usual thing. They wouldn't accept her story—full police prosecution. Remanded for a few weeks. She came in with her husband—he's being supportive but she's in a bit of a state.'

'Any previous form?'

'Oh no. An upright citizen, if ever I met one. I believe her implicitly, as it happens. It's so unfair, Sam!' Her voice rose several notes above its customary calm level. 'Lumping these people in with hardened criminals, and their mistakes with premeditated thefts. Everyone knows how easy it is to do . . . the way the shops are laid out almost invites it . . .'

'I know, I know. Now then, Mrs Barton,' he soothed, 'keep your legendary cool. We can help them best, don't forget, by holding on to our rags when all about us are losing theirs. So,' he went on, leaning back in his chair, folding shirtsleeved arms across his tubby frame, 'what would you have me do?'

'They should qualify for Aid. I think they should have Counsel. Can I ask John Slade? He was really good over that Johnson case.'

'Of course, of course. Go ahead. Give him a buzz on his private line.'

'I've been trying to,' she admitted, 'all morning. But there's no reply.'

'Aha.' He scratched his balding, round head. 'Now I come to think of it, I can explain that. Should have thought of it as soon as you mentioned Slade.'

'What's that?' Gina sat down opposite him, in his clients' chair.

'He ain't there. He's off on a jaunt to the States, I believe—some visiting stunt at a Law School over there—a nice little number, I shouldn't be surprised.' He sighed exaggeratedly. 'They get all the perks, these barristers. Why didn't I listen to my wise old mother? "Sam," she used to say to me . . .'

'Never mind your wise old mother,' his junior partner interrupted rudely. 'What about my clients? Do you think one of John's colleagues would take it on? Richard Noble, for instance—he's usually quite sympathetic to this kind of case. Or what was that Indian chap's name—he was very successful with Mr Hall and his little problem with the umbrella . . .'

'They might.' Sam looked doubtful. 'They're all very busy, but it's well worth a try. Pity about Slade, though,' he mused. 'Would have been ideal for a case like that. Still . . .' he jumped to his feet, making a vague attempt to stack a few papers together among the jungle on his desk, 'doesn't do to brood on what might have been. Try them again after lunch— someone's sure to be there eventually. You have my blessing, Gina—whatever you decide to do, you're sure to do it well.'

She stood up too—reaching to much the same height as him in her stacked heels. 'Thanks, Sam. Have a good lunch—don't imbibe too much. Remember you've got to work this afternoon. Can't have the boss falling asleep at his desk.' She opened the door.

'Me? Imbibe?' he exploded indignantly. 'Never let it be said.' He patted his ample paunch. 'Undernourished, that's what I am. Need all the business lunches I can get—saves Martha from cooking me a meal when I get home.'

She grinned round the door at him before pulling it to behind her.

Within ten minutes, Gina was across the road in the sandwich bar she usually frequented—her gaze fixed on the roaring mass of traffic the other side of the plate-glass window, but her mind wandering far away. Absently nibbling a cheese roll and sipping a glass of apple juice, she failed to notice the tall, thin figure gesticulating at her from the pavement outside. Afraid of making itself conspicuous by its antics, the figure gave up and marched into the bar. It flung its briefcase down on the counter, seating itself on the stool beside her.

'Brian! Where did you spring from? I thought your case was going on all day?'

'So did I. It was adjourned, pending further evidence. So I came back.'

'How's it going?'

Brian Gillow shrugged his narrow, bony shoulders. 'Not too well.' He ran long fingers through his straight, sandy hair; he looked hot and disgruntled. 'It's a knotty one, and no mistake.'

'You look as if you could do with some refreshment,' Gina suggested sympathetically.

'Yes, you're right. Don't go away—I'll just pick something up.' His pale, earnest face became quite good-looking when he smiled, the blue eyes crinkling at the corners.

Although hardly any older than herself, Brian had been with the firm much longer, and was Sam's equal partner—and his exact opposite in almost every respect. Their complementary interests and personalities made for a highly successful balance—and when Gina's own special brand of intuitive circumspection was added to the mix, the team was a force to be reckoned with.

'I won't go anywhere.' She returned the smile. She liked Brian a lot—and he was more than fond of her, she knew that. Given the least encouragement, he could be quite a bit more . . . but she had no intention of offering any such encouragement. Theirs was strictly a working relationship: she had plenty of respect for him as a friend, a companion and a lawyer—but as a man, in the fullest sense, he left her unmoved.

And Gina was in no position to be moved by any man. It was just as well none had come along, in all these years, to undermine her steely resolve to avoid any such involvement, ever again. Once in a lifetime was more than enough. After all, she was still—on paper—a married woman. Brian knew that—as did all the other men who regularly tried to penetrate those defensive layers of armour—and as a weapon, she had found it couldn't be beaten. Flash a wedding ring at them—emphasise the *Mrs* in front of your name—and as often as not they would melt away like snows in spring. There were a few tenacious ones who refused to take the hint—but her standard speech of cool, well-chosen words usually shifted them.

And if that didn't work, as a last resort, she only had to introduce the subject of Toby. His existence rarely failed to shake off even the most clinging admirer. Poor little boy—seven years old and already being used as a bodyguard for his mother. Well, at least he never knew it: determined to keep her professional and private selves entirely distinct, she simply told her colleagues and acquaintances that she had a small child, and then never raised the subject again unless it became absolutely necessary. Their curiosity was often plain in their eyes; but she had to get to know them very well indeed before she confided any more than that.

Brian knew the full story, of course, as did Sam and his wife. She had been with the firm three years now—and when she had joined, only a year had elapsed since Pete had walked out on her. Inevitably, they'd had to know she'd been married, and deserted; that her husband had been an art student—one of those perennial students who look destined to stay that way the rest of their days. During the early years after she had qualified, he had been content to live off her earnings; but then he had fallen for a fellow-student and disappeared out of Gina's life. She hadn't heard so much as a squeak from him for four years.

Divorce would be a simple thing now, she knew that, after all this time. But she clung to the security of the status, the title, of married woman. It was not that she wanted Pete back—far from it: she had got well-used to being without him. In fact, having him back now was the last thing she would have wanted. No, it was just the safety she felt it gave her—keeping those other predators, as she saw them, at bay; reminding her constantly that her first duty was to little Toby.

She had met Pete while she was still at University. Theirs had been a whirlwind romance: nineteen years old, beautiful and impressionable, she had offered him all her innocence, her shrewd intelligence, her loyalty—without question. She was certain she was doing the right thing, although she had been cautiously warned off by concerned family and friends. He might be handsome, dashing, artistic, sensitive, they said; his *mañana* attitude might be endearing, his childlike charm attractive—but he would let her down, they prophesied, as sure as eggs. She had merely smiled her gentle smile, refusing to believe it of him. She was deeply in love—and so, to be fair, was he . . . but, as she had learned painfully since, there are degrees of depth in love; and some people are only capable of the most shallow of them.

Sexually, it had been exciting. He had taught her sensuality, made her aware of the powerful links between physical and emotional satisfaction. Otherwise they had little shared experience. By the time she obtained her degree, at twenty-one, and articled herself to a practising solicitor, they had begun to drift apart. And just at that crucial moment—perhaps in a vain attempt to renew a failing bond—Toby had made his appearance.

Gina had refused to give up her budding career, and Pete had supported her decision: after all, it provided an easy living for him. He stayed at home, working on paintings that never seemed to reach fruition—and looking after the baby in his somewhat haphazard fashion. When he had to go into college, he simply took Toby with him and deposited him in the crêche provided—where, Gina knew, he would be safe, at least. It was far from an ideal arrangement, but it seemed to work out all right; they muddled through from week to week.

Then, one day when Toby was just three years old and Gina was settling into her first proper job, Pete announced abruptly that he was leaving. He had fallen irrevocably in love, he said, with a girl at the college. He was sorry to leave Toby, of course; but there it was—he was probably going to Cuba to start a new life, so Toby would have to be sacrificed. He hoped Gina would understand: he had loved her, she must believe that, but her 'straight' kind of life was not for him. He was sure she'd be happier too, if she thought it through. They never had had much in common, apart from Toby—and their initial passion for each other, which was, he pointed out, decidedly on the wane after five years.

One part of her wasn't surprised; several parts even understood. Nonetheless the shock was considerable, and she had fled to her parents for temporary emotional support. To their eternal credit, not a single 'I told you so' ever passed their lips: she would always be grateful to them for their restraint.

Eventually, strengthening her will, she had returned to London and carried on with her life. It hadn't been so difficult, really, apart from the complex arrangements that had to be made about caring for Toby. Financially, she was secure; she enjoyed her work—and joining Goldman and Gillow turned out to be the best move she ever made.

And now, three years on, here was Gillow himself,

advancing in her direction with a ham salad and a cup
of coffee. He sat down next to her. 'Well—how are
things?' he enquired, loading his fork. 'Anything new
and exciting?'

'Not really. Another shoplifting case.'

'Another?' He frowned. 'Seems to be an epidemic.
What's the score this time?'

Once again she described the unfortunate experience
of Peggy Haines. 'I wanted John Slade in on it, but
Sam tells me he's away, so I thought maybe Richard
or one of the other partners . . .'

Brian chewed thoughtfully. 'Got a new man in those
Chambers, I heard today. Did Sam tell you?'

'No—I don't think he knew. Is he likely to have his
heart in the right place, whoever he is? Not a lot of
money in cases like the Haines'.'

'I've got no idea. All I've heard is, he's a wild
Welshman, just arrived back after a spell in Cardiff.
He was called to the Bar up here years ago, then went
home to practise—now decided to make a come-back
on the big scene, for some reason. You never know—
he might be just the man you need for this case. If he's
on Slade's Chambers, he must be okay.'

'I suppose so. What's his name?'

'Oh, what was it . . . something ridiculously Welsh,
I remember that . . . Rees, that was it,' he announced
triumphantly. 'Dai Rees.'

'Dai?' Gina's brow wrinkled expressively. '*Dai?*'

'Yes, Dai—you know—short for David. Or, no
doubt, if he's that ethnic, *Dafydd*.' Satirically, he gave
the name its Welsh pronunciation.

'I didn't think people outside the Valleys—and
Welsh jokes—really called themselves Dai,' she
reflected. 'I wonder what he's like?'

'I've heard he's stunning in Court—a real power-
packed Celt. But if you get him on to this case of
yours,' Brian pointed out, 'you'll doubtless discover
for yourself. I'm afraid I can't enlighten you any
further.' He drained his coffee. 'Coming over? I told

today's client to come and see me—he'll be arriving——' he glanced at his watch, 'five minutes ago.' He smiled wearily. 'No let-up in this game, is there?'

They paid for their lunch and crossed the busy main road together. 'Free for dinner one evening next week?' he asked as they approached the wide glass doors. It was an invitation he attempted once a week, on average; and about once a month she accepted it, and they had a companionable meal, or occasionally went to see a play.

'Not next week, Brian,' she apologised. 'Maybe the one after?'

'Maybe,' he agreed—never pushing, always easy-going, passive. Much as he might secretly wish he could get further with her, he lacked the drive to do anything about it. She was well aware of that—and it suited her fine. 'Well, see you later,' he said. 'Good luck with the Celtic Fringes,' he added with a grin.

CHAPTER TWO

As soon as she was back at her desk, Gina tried John Slade's Chambers again—but this time she dialled the general office number, rather than the private one which by-passed the switchboard to reach direct to any of the barristers who happened to be there.

The clerk who answered spoke in the bored tones of one who has said the same words a dozen times that day already. 'I'm afraid Mr Slade is not here. He is in America.'

'I know,' Gina replied. 'I was wondering if I could speak to Richard Noble?'

'He's away too—on Circuit in the Midlands. Won't be back for a fortnight.'

'I see.' She thought quickly. 'How about Mr Singh?'

'At Court all day today, Miss,' the clerk apologised. 'And the rest of the week too. And probably next week as well, by the look of things. No, the only Counsel here this afternoon is Mr Rees. He's a new member, recently arrived from . . .'

'Yes, I know who he is,' Gina assured him. 'I'd better have a word with him then, I suppose,' she decided, with an unaccountable reluctance. At least she knew all the others personally, and it was difficult, briefing a total stranger.

'Who shall I say is calling, Miss?'

'He won't know me from Eve, but it's Gina Barton, of Goldman and Gillow.'

'Very well, Miss Barton.'

After a short pause, during which the line regaled her with its usual esoteric clicks and buzzes, the earpiece resounded to a single barked monosyllable. 'Yes?'

'Er—Mr Rees?'

'Speaking. And you, I am informed, are Gina Barton of Goldman and Gillow?'

'That's right. You won't have heard of me, but . . .'

'On the contrary, Miss Barton, I am fully appraised of your existence. I have before me, as it happens, a stack of files representing cases of yours—briefs which I appear to have inherited from my good friend and colleague, John Slade. I was just in the process of wading through them. You could hardly have phoned at a more opportune moment.'

The voice held clear, confident authority; but it was also rich, deep and tuneful with its lilting Welsh inflexions. '*Mrs* Barton,' she found herself correcting automatically—hardly aware of the subconscious need, even at this distance, to underline her defences. 'Are you having problems with them then, Mr Rees?'

'I do not often have . . . problems with understanding briefs which are put before me, *Mrs* Barton,' he countered instantly. 'And these are admirably concise and detailed. No, but I do like to read between the lines—get to the real meat inside the story. For that reason, I find, it is usually necessary to discuss a case at first hand with the briefing solicitor, and preferably the clients as well. Are you free to come round for that purpose?'

He was certainly not a man to waste time on unnecessary ceremony. Gina felt distinctly breathless; if he was like this on the telephone, what would he be like in the flesh? 'You don't mean now?'

'I do mean now. As I say, you've caught me at a good time. Tomorrow and the next day I shall be in Court. Next week looks pretty full, too. I've hardly arrived in the Great City, but it seems I've joined an exceptionally active Chambers.'

And your reputation has doubtless spread before you, Gina's mind added; but she didn't say it. She had a hunch that a boost was the last thing his ego required. 'Well—I'm not sure,' she began doubtfully,

instead. 'I've got a pile of conveyancing to get through
... but there is a new case I'd like to ask you about.
It's rather important ... that's why I 'phoned ...'

'Well, don't dither, young lady. Make up your
mind. I'm a busy fellow, you know. Come over if you
can. Where are you—let me see ...' there was a
rustling of papers. 'King's Cross area, isn't that right?'

'That is correct.' She cringed, almost speechless
with anger; how dare he adopt this insultingly
patronising tone with her? She was no junior clerk—it
would have been bad enough if she had been—but a
fully fledged professional solicitor. If she hadn't been
female, she suspected, his attitude might have been
extremely different.

'Are you mobile?' he demanded bluntly.

'I drive a car, if that's what you mean,' she
conceded stiffly.

'Have you got it with you now?'

'I did bring it to work this morning, yes.'

'Well then—it's a ten-minute trip. Why don't you
pop over in half-an-hour or so; then we can go
through these cases quickly, and you can tell me about
your new one? Otherwise,' he pointed out logically, 'it
looks as though it might be weeks before we get
another chance, and if it's a pressing matter ...'

Gina swallowed her pride. For the sake of Peggy
Haines, she would go. There were no actual
appointments this afternoon, and the conveyancing
could wait. It bored her to tears, anyway, but it had to
be done: property transactions were the bread-and-
butter of their work, as they were of most solicitors'
firms. 'Very well, Mr Rees. I'll be there in half-an-
hour.'

'You know where it is?'

'I should do,' she returned tautly, 'I've been there
often enough.'

'Good. I'll tell them to reserve you a parking space
downstairs.' They would, too, she thought—he was
the kind of man whose requests were more like

summary instructions—which, she was certain, most people would jump to obey. Look at her, for instance: she wasn't in the habit of setting out at a moment's notice to suit the convenience of a professional colleague she had never so much as set eyes on. 'See you soon, then, *Mrs* Barton,' he went on. She wondered if she was imagining the slight edge of mockery in his tone as he deliberately emphasised her married status: it made her feel oddly insecure.

As soon as he had rung off, she pressed her buzzer to contact the secretary. 'Can you let me have all the files on clients we've recently briefed John Slade about, please, Michele? And check with Mr Goldman that it's okay if I go over to Lincoln's Inn—the new Counsel there wants further briefing on some of them. Tell him I'll take that new case with me, the one I was telling him about earlier—and I shouldn't be away long.'

'That's fine, Mrs Barton,' the message came back a few minutes later. 'The files are ready when you are.'

'Thanks, Michele. If anyone calls me, ask them to try again later.'

It was always striking to enter the hallowed precincts of any of the four Inns of Court. She drove now through the ancient stone gateway from Lincoln's Inn Fields, past the gate porter (who waved her in from his bothy with a smile, recognising her by now), into the placid, solid collegiate atmosphere of the Inn itself—which had surely remained for many centuries exactly as it was today: an undisturbed haven of civilised tranquillity right at the very heart of brash commercial London. As Gina parked and locked her white Metro, she marvelled yet again at the slightly crumbling Gothic dignity of the buildings themselves. The place was an island, she always thought, belonging in another age—an anachronistic backwater, set in its sea of rolling, close-cropped lawns.

She had had reason to visit them all, of course, over

the years: Lincoln's and Gray's Inns, the Middle and Inner Temples; but she probably knew this one best, for the simple reason that the firm used these particular Chambers most often. Each Inn dated back to mediaeval times, she knew—with its own distinct, cherished traditions and history. For a short time, once in a while, it was pleasant to escape the pace of real life in their slow formality; but she was usually glad enough to get out again in the end, and back to that bustling reality outside.

The first thing that struck her today, on entering John Slade's Chambers, was that the man sitting behind John Slade's massive desk was apparently the exact and total antithesis of John Slade. Slightly built, fair and dapper, John was always soft-spoken, under-stated, polite and rational. He treated everyone—whatever their class or gender—with equally charming courtesy. It was difficult to realise that beneath the well-bred public school accent there lurked an egalitarian heart which rejoiced in overturning some of society's more pointlessly orthodox whims and regulations.

The person she was faced with now dominated the spacious room, even from his seated position, just as his tones had dominated the telephone receiver—exuding confidence and charisma. He was big—broad-backed and burly—perhaps the son of agricultural or mining stock. No expensively cut suit was going to disguise that muscular frame as anything other than it powerfully was: an aggressively virile, essentially male, body.

As Gina hesitated in the doorway—her briefcase under one arm, her leather bag hanging from the other shoulder by its long strap—she took in all these details almost subliminally with her trained, lawyer's eye. More immediately she was aware of the top of his head, bent over a pile of documents in which he was obviously immersed. A strong black mane curled over it in vigorous disorder—anarchic, unruly. More than

likely, her mind suggested as she gazed at it, these
were characteristics shared by the man himself. She
remembered Brian's words, just an hour ago—*a wild
Welshman*, he had said; and what was that other
expression?—*a power-packed Celt*. Well, even sitting
quietly at a desk, these epithets fitted him perfectly:
she could imagine just how imposing he would be,
standing up in Court, with that dark, lyrical voice and
powerful presence.

He was fully aware of her own presence at that
moment, she knew; but he took his time, deliberately
finishing what he was doing before he acknowledged
it. That was all one with the arrogance he had
displayed on the 'phone, and she cringed again,
recalling their recent conversation. This was the sort
of man who was the centre of his own universe—and
uncompromisingly expected to be at the hub of
everyone else's as well. She had met his kind before,
and she wasn't daunted by them. They usually
responded, eventually, to a dose of judicious female
manipulation: not the sort of idiotic behaviour most
often implied by that expression—Gina had no time
for feminine wiles of that nature—no, it was
something far more secret and subtle which she had in
mind.

She waited patiently until he saw fit to look up.
When he did, she all but gasped audibly under the
impact of his eyes, but caught herself in the nick of
time. They came as a shock, because they were wide-
set and light—a clear, cool grey—in stark contrast to
the midnight blackness of his hair, the swarthiness of
his skin. His other features were as forceful as the rest
of him: long straight nose, square thrusting jaw, firmly
moulded mouth. She could appreciate their effect on
one level; but kept herself detached, making sure that
her reaction was purely objective . . . a process she had
become expert at over the years.

It needed all that accumulated expertise to hold his
piercing, lucid gaze with her own serene honey-brown

one. But she returned his scrutiny, measure for measure. 'Mrs Barton, I presume?' His frank investigation now incorporated the rest of her figure—blatantly taking it all in, but giving nothing away. She wondered, despite herself, whether he was liking what he saw. He waved a large impatient hand towards the chair opposite him. 'Come in, come in, sit down. Don't . . . lurk. I can't abide people who lurk.'

With dignity, taking her time, she approached the desk. 'How do you do, Mr Rees.' It was important to observe the formalities—hold on to the predictable structures of polite behaviour.

His dark eyebrows registered brief surprise, then satirical humour. Standing up, towering over her by at least nine inches, he stretched out his right hand across the desk-top. Square-cut, broad fingers enclosed her own small ones in a firm dry grasp. 'Mrs Barton,' he murmured, 'the pleasure is all mine.' Then, unceremoniously, he sat down again; and so did she. 'Well now,' he went on, touching the tips of those wide fingers together, 'my time is precious—as, I am quite sure, is yours. So, shall we get straight down to business? Do you wish to deal with these established cases of yours first?'

Gina was already unloading the stack of files from her briefcase and laying them briskly down on the polished expanse of mahogany which separated her from him. She concentrated hard as she did so—refusing to look up and meet that sardonic gaze. 'Fine by me,' she replied. 'Here they all are—I think I should be able to direct your attention . . . between the lines of most of them.'

'Good, good. I like an organised, efficient lady. And what a bonus if she's a decorative one as well.'

Taken off guard, she glanced up sharply—in time to catch a glint from the grey eyes. Fighting the blush which treacherously threatened to invade her face and neck—something which wasn't supposed to happen to her any more—she opened the top file and adopted her most businesslike manner. 'Now this gentleman is in a most interesting situation . . .' she began, in a slightly husky tone.

He grinned; then, rummaging through his own files until he located his notes on the same case, he listened intently to what she had to say. His mind was totally alert; its quicksilver agility missed nothing—no nuance, no subtlety. She had never encountered anything quite like it, in all her experience of sharp-witted lawyers. By the time they had gone through the whole pile of cases, he was fully versed in every detail of each one—and could, she was sure, have dealt with any of them in Court comprehensively at that very moment, had he been called upon to do so.

After forty minutes of keeping up with him, she might have expected to feel exhausted, or at least enervated; but her own mental processes were far from dull, and she found that the interaction had filled her with a sense of exhilaration. His company was a challenge: there was no denying that. Both physically and intellectually, he was the most stimulating man she had met in a long time—probably ever. But he carried strong undercurrents along with him, of risk—even of danger. Gina was acute enough to understand that any challenge is always dangerous—the excitement it generates being inextricably linked with the risk.

'Well, Mrs Barton. I think that about ties those up, don't you? We appear to constitute an excellent team, wouldn't you say? I'm sure that between us we can achieve satisfactory results for these clients of yours.' Dai Rees leaned expansively back in his chair, fingertips pressed together in front of his broad chest in a gesture which Gina already recognised. He surveyed her unblinkingly for several seconds with an intensity that was almost fierce; then his expression lightened into an unexpectedly boyish grin. 'How about a cup of tea? Shall I ask old Perks to send some in?'

'Not for me thanks, Mr Rees.' She was still on her

guard—cautious, reserved. 'I'm rather concerned to get on to this other case, if you don't mind. I don't usually press things forward in such a hurry, but this one has been remanded surprisingly quickly and I feel . . .'

He expelled an ostentatiously deep sigh. 'No peace for the wicked. No rest for the weary. Are you always such a hard taskmistress, Mrs Barton? Do you wield such iron authority over your own family?' When she failed to respond to this unnecessarily personal query, he intruded even further into her private life. 'I assume you do have a family, as well as a fortunate young husband to return to every evening? I'm not sure what it is about you . . .' he regarded her quizzically, dark head on one side, 'but there's something maternal there somewhere, under the veneer of . . . unapproachability. Something of the— the Lady Madonna; the Virtuous Mother. Am I right,' he concluded—triumphant in the secure knowledge that he usually was, 'or am I right?'

'I do have a child, yes.' She made the statement as reluctantly as if she was confessing some shameful vice. 'And I can hardly deny that that makes me a mother.'

'There you are—told you so.' He was so pleased with himself, she could have kicked him; but she did nothing so unsuitable. Instead, she pointed to the Haines folder, now open on the desk. 'Mr Rees. I have to get back to the office. Mr Goldman will be expecting me. Could we please . . .?'

'*Mr* Goldman, is it? And *Mr* Gillow, too?' he interrupted mockingly. 'Surely the estimable Gillow and Goldman do not expect such formality from their junior partner—not assistant, I note, but full partner in crime? I've only known you five minutes but I was about to make so bold as to suggest demotion—or is it promotion—to the use of given names. Could you bring yourself to call me Dai?'

Her reaction was cold. 'I'd rather not, if you don't

mind.' This had gone quite far enough—considerably
too far—for a first meeting. And if she had much to do
with it, there would not be many more meetings; he
made her feel distinctly uneasy.

His eyebrows shot upwards. 'Just as you wish, Gina
Barton. So, about this case of yours. If I can detain
you no further with offers of sustenance or social
pleasantries, we must return to the job in hand. What
does it concern?'

'It's a shoplifting case,' she told him, relieved to get
back on to neutral territory.

He groaned. 'Those, I can do without. They are
never straightforward, and in my opinion there are a
good deal too many of them around. Never mind.' He
leaned over the desk in order to see the documents.
'Give it to me with both barrels. I can take it.'

This wasn't a promising start; but Gina took a deep
breath. 'It concerns a woman who . . .'

'Don't tell me,' he cut in, clutching his forehead in
satirical despair. 'Not another of these bored meno-
pausal matrons caught out depriving some unfortunate
department store of its lawful property?'

Gina raised horrified eyes to study his face. She had
hardly expected a reaction like this; she sensed an
imminent confrontation. She forced herself to stay
cool, to make sure she had heard him correctly before
she made a response to the piece of outright prejudice
she had just witnessed. 'I beg your pardon?'

'You heard me, Mrs Barton,' he replied levelly. 'I'm
getting fed up with tales like this—cropping up
everywhere—moments of aberration, errors of judgment, call them what you will—they appear to be
almost universally perpetrated by women who have
nothing better to do, and who then choose to blame
their little slips on some major hormonal upheaval: the
Time of Life, the Time of Month, pregnancy, or some
other Female Complaint . . .'

Gina had heard more than enough. She drew herself
up to face him, squaring her shoulders, tilting her chin

defiantly. 'Mr Rees, you must be teasing me. You are aware, surely, that you're talking in ludicrous sexist generalisations?'

Once again, surprise flickered in his eyes, but almost at once they became a practised mask. 'That's a matter of opinion; it's what I happen to think. You can take it or leave it, Mrs Barton. Naturally, that doesn't mean I won't defend your client. I've done it before, many times—successfully too, against all the odds—and I'll do it again. But there is a strong tendency, I find, for our Learned Friends on the Bench to share my point of view.'

'That,' Gina pointed out haughtily, 'could be because almost all of them are men.'

'Be that as it may,' he shrugged, 'if I refused every brief which I didn't feel happy about, ideologically speaking, I'd have chalked up a lot less experience in Court than I have. I was merely airing my own personal views to you, as an individual. Of course they would not influence my professional handling of the matter in any way.'

'They couldn't help but influence it,' Gina objected heatedly. 'I don't see how you can possibly take it on, feeling as you do—or,' she added with even greater vehemence, 'how I can possibly let you.'

Again he gave that nonchalant shrug, but the light of battle was in his eyes. He was a barrister, after all: there was nothing he would enjoy more than a good argument. Debating was what they were supremely fitted for. Gina appreciated a discussion herself, but this subject went much too deep to cause her anything but blind rage. 'There's no compulsion,' he reminded her lightly. 'I'm here, offering to take the brief, if that's what you want. Assuming you want the best for you client, I advise you to accept. With Slade away, I doubt whether anyone else here would be willing or able—they're all snowed under with work. So—it seems you're down to yours truly; or looking elsewhere.'

He had a point; and Gina was in no mood or position to start chasing round other contacts to find a good Counsel—not for a relatively insignificant case like this, in a Minor Court. Not that it was insignificant, of course, to Peggy and Jim Haines— anything but. Making a great effort, she tried sweet reason. 'If you really believe those things you've just said, Mr Rees—if you didn't say them just to . . . test me . . . get a reaction . . .?'

'Now why,' he cut in smoothly, 'should I want to do a thing like that?'

She stuck to her guns. '. . . if you won't allow that women do have—certain times when they are less—in control than at other times . . .'

'Yes?' he prompted impatiently, as she paused to choose her words with care.

'Then to what *do* you attribute such common moments of weakness, absent-mindedness? Because they are very common, you know.'

'Why can't they be just plain, simple moments of weakness and absent-mindedness? Does there always have to be a more profound explanation—domestic circumstances, chemistry?' he demanded. 'Men have to take the full rap for their little stupidities; why shouldn't women?'

'Of course they should. It wasn't me,' she reminded him tautly, 'who first mentioned the . . . hormonal aspect; it was you. As a matter of fact, I wasn't going to, and I was surprised when you did.'

'Well, that makes a change,' he countered rudely. 'So, what are we arguing about?'

She struggled to control her exasperation. 'I agree that the sort of . . . more personal explanations you described are only ever part of the story—though often quite a major part,' she maintained emphatically. 'But if you've got so little time for them, how do you account for the fact that this particular unpleasant experience seems to happen so much more often to women than it does to men?'

He was more than ready for that one. 'Women's innate foolishness, of course. Scatty creatures, you ladies, bless you. Lovely, but empty-headed—apart from certain notable exceptions, naturally,' he added with an ingratiating bow in her direction, 'which are all the more refreshing to encounter.'

Gina was very far from mollified at being singled out as one of the few. 'You can't mean that?' She banged her fist down on the desk, now losing her temper completely. 'I never thought I'd actually hear anyone saying that, and meaning it. I've always despised strident feminists . . .'

'I should think so too,' he remarked blandly.

She ignored the interruption. '. . . but faced with a man like you, I can fully understand their point of view. With all your education and intelligence, you must know perfectly well that there's nothing intrinsically . . . scattier, or more foolish or empty-headed about women than there is about men. There may be a certain feminine image which has been projected over the years, mostly by men . . .'

'No smoke without fire,' he intoned complacently.

'But surely absent-mindedness is not a prerogative of the female sex?' She was now well and truly into her stride. 'Men are no less capable of . . . stupidities. You've just said so yourself,' she recalled triumphantly.

'And you yourself have just pointed out, Mrs Barton, that lapses of this kind appear to inflict your own sex considerably more often, statistically, than mine.'

'Perhaps,' she retorted at once, 'that's because they get landed with doing nearly all the shopping.'

'Touché.' He inclined his head graciously to accept the point. 'However, I stand by my thesis that most women are, by their very nature, less controlled, more subjective, more liable to get carried away in the heat of the moment—and are more dominated by their emotions than most men are. It's perfectly simple; you don't need to look for complicated biological or psychological excuses. Why bother?' he went on irritatingly, before she could answer. 'We love you just the way you are. Go on being your unpredictable selves, and help make the world go round.'

'And what are we supposed to do,' Gina muttered, teeth and fists clenched, 'when we are arrested, and our whole lives turned upside-down, as a result of some piece of—of endearingly fluffy-headed *unpredictability*?' She spat out the word, as if it was the ultimate in insults. 'Perhaps, if women are the foolish little creatures you seem to think, we shouldn't even be allowed in shops at all? Maybe we shouldn't be allowed out of the house—for our own safety and the better management of the world out here?'

'Oh, I wouldn't go quite as far as that,' he drawled. 'The world would be a dull place indeed without female company gracing it. Don't get me wrong—I'm a great fan of the female gender. Some of my best friends,' he assured her gravely, 'are women.' She wondered if he had a wife, and if so, what the poor woman thought of his views; her heart went out to anyone who had to actually live with a man like this. 'No,' he went on, 'I wasn't suggesting a system of *purdah*. Don't think I'd like that at all.'

'I'm relieved to hear it.' For a moment she sat silent, collecting her scattered poise. Suddenly it seemed pointless to continue with this interview. 'Well, Mr Rees.' She rose to her feet, gathering her papers together. 'I don't think I need to keep you any longer.'

'But you haven't briefed me about this case yet,' he protested. 'Come on now, Mrs Barton, surely you're not going to take umbrage and let your clients suffer just because I was indiscreet enough to share a private opinion with you? That would be a most . . . irrational reaction, and if I may say so——' he smiled sarcastically, 'very female.'

Gina winced at this uncalled-for twist of the knife.

'You have a perfect right to your opinions, Mr Rees. And I reserve the right to brief whichever Counsel I choose. After what I've heard today, there's no way I could allow you to take this case on.'

'Are you normally this stubborn?' he enquired mildly.

'Not stubborn. Just ... principled,' she replied, avoiding his eyes.

He stood up; she refused to be daunted by the sheer size of him. 'I've said nothing revolutionary; nothing you wouldn't find most people agreeing with, if they were honest with themselves.'

'Most men, you mean.' She glared at him. 'Are you trying to tell me that you never make foolish mistakes, Mr Rees? Never indulge in moments of weakness? Never admit to moments of absent-mindedness?'

It didn't take him long to consider that. 'I think I can safely say I don't.' He considered again. 'No, not really. I wouldn't be much of an advocate if I was easily swayed, or diverted.'

'Perhaps not in your professional life, but what about your personal life? Surely you must occasionally allow your ... total male mastery of the situation to slip, just a little?' she taunted.

'I don't think so, Mrs Barton.' The grey eyes were steely now, hard. 'No, I think not.'

She spread her fingers in a gesture of resignation. Then, briskly, she clicked the lock of her briefcase and pushed back her chair. 'Then there's nothing more to be said.'

'Mrs Barton,' he said, and the musical voice was low, persuasive, 'can't we be adults about this? I've got all your other cases well-briefed; won't you let me add this one? You haven't even told me the story.'

'I don't intend to. With your attitude, it would be a waste of breath.'

'But suppose,' he suggested calmly, 'you don't find another Counsel willing to take it? Presumably your clients have expressed a specific desire to be represented in Court?'

Her gold-brown eyes looked straight into his. 'In that case, Mr Rees,' she declared, turning to leave, 'I shall represent them myself.'

CHAPTER THREE

IT was later than usual by the time Gina got away from the office. The visit to Lincoln's Inn had taken up a lot more of the afternoon than she had intended—especially once she had stopped seething and recovered her normal level of poise sufficiently to carry on with everyday work.

At six o'clock she was parking her car outside a tall Georgian terraced house in a peaceful street in inner North London. The area was central enough to be dominated by yellow lines and parking meters, so her windscreen displayed a Resident's Permit which allowed her to use the marked-out space reserved for the purpose along one side of the road.

Gina and Toby occupied the bottom half of the four-storey house. Given the choice, she might have preferred to live higher up, enjoying the sense of space afforded by sweeping views across London and Regent's Park; but she had deliberately chosen the lower maisonette when Toby was a toddler, faced with problems of hoisting him and his push-chair up several flights of stairs. She was doubly glad, now, that she'd made that decision: a decent-sized garden went with the flat, and in summer both she and Toby made full use of it. She had dug him a sandpit, and bought him a small climbing frame as soon as he was old enough to scramble about. This status symbol made him popular with his friends, who often came round to visit at weekends.

She locked up the car, but she didn't go straight into the house. Instead, she walked fifty yards down the road until she came to another very like it—perhaps smarter and better maintained, but basically identical. Climbing the few steps to its varnished pine door, she rang the bell.

At once, childish squeaks and energetic footsteps made themselves heard on the other side of the door, which was flung open to reveal two short figures jostling each other in the wide hall. One of them hurled itself at her, almost knocking the briefcase out of her arms.

'Mummy! You're late! Jackie says I can stay a bit longer, because we're watching a brilliant thing on telly. Can I still stay, even though you're here now? Please, Mummy, can I?'

After returning his warm hug, she extricated herself from the exuberant embrace. 'I don't know, Toby. Give me a chance to talk to Jackie first.' Smiling at her son, she felt her chest tighten, as it always did at the sight of his limpid brown eyes and glossy fair curls. Pete had been blond, with blue eyes; she herself came from a darker-skinned family—and the combined result was striking in Toby.

She turned to his companion, a boy of much the same age, with a carrot-orange thatch and a liberal sprinkling of freckles. 'Hallo, Joe. Where's your mum?'

'In the kitchen. She says you're to go in. Come on,' he ordered, turning to lead the way, pulling at his friend's arm. 'Come on, Tobe. Let's see the rest of that programme.'

Toby looked uncertainly at his mother. 'Can I finish watching it? It's a fantastic programme, Mum. You see, there are these monsters, and they . . .'

'Okay, okay,' she laughed. 'Just as long as you come when I call. I dare say Jackie's had more than enough of you for one afternoon.'

'Great; thanks, Mum.' He followed Joe upstairs in the direction of the playroom, which was where the children's television held court. Jackie and her husband James, a successful advertising consultant, owned the whole of the house and could afford to allow their small family to spread.

Obeying Joe's terse instructions, Gina found her friend in the large, orderly kitchen, putting finishing touches to an appetising array of pies and flans. A pretty floral apron covered her jeans and cotton shirt; her short, shining auburn hair was neat as ever. Jackie was a home-body, and happy to be one: always busy, always creative, and—as far as Gina could see—almost always content. It was just as well she did feel like that: James undertook plenty of entertaining in the course of his job, and Jackie made an excellent hostess.

Gina was never sure whether she pitied the other woman or envied her situation. She knew she wouldn't like to be some man's . . . adjunct; an auxiliary, rather than a working person in her own right—but then again, when she was honest with herself she had to admit it would be rather nice to have that security; not to have to rush about being provider and parent, housekeeper and breadwinner all at once.

She grinned at Jackie now as she sank gratefully into one of the polished wooden chairs drawn up at the matching table. 'Sorry I'm late, Jackie. Got a bit . . . behind today. I decided not to 'phone and make myself even later.'

Jackie returned the grin as she filled the electric kettle. 'Don't be so silly. It's no more than half-an-hour later than usual, and anyway I don't mind a bit. I always let you know in advance if there's something urgent on. He's no trouble, you know that; in fact you're doing me a favour because Joe's a hundred per cent easier to manage when Toby's here.'

'Bless you. Still, I don't like to—I like to keep to our arrangements . . .' Gina knew it was true about Joe, who was a volatile, temperamental child—all moods and fancies to match his red hair. His older brother Ben—dark, like his father, and already at secondary school—was as serious and studious as Joe was extrovert.

Jackie leaned on the draining board, looking directly at Gina for the first time. 'Had a hard day?' she asked sympathetically. 'Looks as if you can do with a cup of tea—it'll be ready in a minute.'

'Not the best day I've lived through,' Gina admitted. 'A cup of tea will be magic—if you're sure you've got time. I'll take Toby off at once if . . .'

'Do stop being so jumpy,' Jackie admonished. 'You know I'd say if I wanted you to go. As it happens, I'm really glad to see you; I've been slaving over a hot stove all day, and a bit of intelligent adult company is definitely called for.'

'Don't know how intelligent I can promise to be.' Gina yawned. 'Are all these goodies for the freezer, or are you expecting a few hundred visitors?'

'Well, stocks are getting a bit low . . . but as a matter of fact we have got a party coming up soon. I do like to be organised well in advance.' She poured boiling water into the teapot. 'Things tend to creep up on you otherwise.'

'I admire your efficiency, Jackie. I don't know how you do it.'

'You don't know how *I* do it!' the other woman retorted. 'Who's the one with the challenging job, whose home is always tidy, whose son is always a model of sweetness and civilised behaviour? And all that without . . .' Glancing at her friend, she turned her back to reach for a biscuit tin from the cupboard.

'Without benefit of male support?' supplied Gina, caustically.

'Without any support,' Jackie amended firmly.

'Nonsense. Of course I have support. I couldn't do it without you, for a start. If you didn't collect Toby from school every day and keep him here till I got back—and even have him in the holidays a good bit of the time . . .'

'I've just said, it's no problem for me; it helps me, and I like it. I'm very fond of Toby, Gina. He's a darling. Anyway,' she added, bending down to get the milk out of the fridge, 'it's a salve to my conscience.'

'It's what?' Gina frowned, puzzled.

'It makes me feel less guilty about my own situation

. . . everything I've got to be thankful for. It's a way of showing solidarity—you know . . .'

'With the sisterhood?' Gina smiled.

'Something like that. I mean, I don't do much for other people. The least I can do, it seems to me, is help out a woman friend who needs it.' She poured tea into two willow-patterned cups.

'Well, whatever your deeper motives, you know I really appreciate it. My life would have been an endless series of complications without you: au pairs, nannies . . . goodness knows how I'd have coped these last three years. As it is . . .'

'As it is,' Jackie pointed out, 'I've got an au pair, a cleaning lady, no job, an enormous house, and no . . . financial worries. And everything I need including a wonderful husband. So there you are. Not that I regard any of those as an automatic prerequisite for a satisfying life,' she assured Gina hastily.

'Not even the wonderful husband?' Gina teased, feeling herself relax at last as she sipped the aromatic brew.

'Certainly not,' declared Jackie, who adored her husband, and—as Gina well knew—was equally adored in return. 'Anyway,' she went on archly, 'I'm well aware of your opinion of the opposite sex. There wouldn't be a lot of point trying to convert you.'

'Not a lot,' Gina agreed bluntly, 'especially today.'

Jackie's auburn eyebrows lifted. 'Why not today, especially?'

Gina sighed. 'Oh, nothing really. I had an altercation with a prime example of the species this afternoon. A real, rare, rootin'-tootin', fully paid-up member of the MCP brigade.'

'Sounds fascinating. Tell me more. You career girls get all the breaks.'

'Don't you believe it. The only thing liable to break after this episode was my legendary veneer of calm. In fact,' she confessed ruefully, grimacing at the memory, 'it did.'

'You? You lost your cool? Really?' Jackie settled

herself down with her tea in the chair opposite, her green eyes alert with interest. 'This I must hear. The man who can cause our Gina's blood pressure to rocket must be a real stinker.'

'He is,' Gina told her grimly.

'But who is he? How did you meet him? In which of your many capacities did you encounter this . . . fiend in masculine shape? Come on, Gina,' she encouraged, as her friend showed signs of reluctance to pursue the fascinating subject. 'I'm a lonely, trapped housewife, remember? Stuck in the kitchen all day with only the radio for company? In desperate need of a breath of fresh air from the big bad outside world? Share your exotic, sophisticated life with me . . . go on.'

Gina laughed outright. 'There's nothing exotic or sophisticated about this business, I can tell you. This was one bit of excitement I could have done without.'

'Well, tell me anyway,' Jackie wheedled. 'It might help your blood pressure.'

'It's just this barrister I met today, that's all. I was about to instruct him on a shoplifting case—this woman who'd been arrested in Oxford Street . . .' and she proceeded to outline the details of Peggy Haines's experience.

Jackie, sidetracked from the original issue, was overcome with compassion. 'Oh, the poor thing. God, when I think of the times I've nearly done that. Once I actually did,' she recalled. 'A long time ago I bought a birthday card at a stationer's, and there was another one stuck to it, underneath. I only paid for the one but when I got home I found I had two.'

'Did you take it back?'

'Blow that—of course I didn't! That would have looked awful. No, I just kept it and used it—and I've been nursing the guilty secret ever since. Till now,' she grinned, 'I've unburdened it to you.'

'Well, it's not quite the same; but if you'd been picked up you might have been prosecuted too. That just goes to show how easily done it is. Anyway, so I went to this barrister, and he . . .'

'Oh yes. The monstrous chauvinist. Don't tell me—he blamed it all on the poor lady's hormones? That makes me so mad . . .'

'Quite the opposite,' Gina explained. 'He took the line that women have no excuse for such stupidities except being scattier, shallower, more emotional than men. The female of the species, according to this gentleman, is hardly safe to be allowed out on the streets, and only should be because otherwise life would be so dull and drab for the male. I tell you, Jackie . . .' her colour rose and she tensed up just thinking about it, 'I was so furious, I could have hit him!'

'Perhaps you should have done. Sometimes they're only doing it for effect, like naughty boys. Like Joe,' she said thoughtfully. 'I've never given him a good smack, but James has, and I sometimes wonder if it isn't what he needs.'

'Trouble with this one is, he's one of those well-built types—you know, all macho arrogance and aggression—and I didn't fancy my chances if he got . . . well . . .'

'Roused?' Jackie leaned over to scrutinise her more closely. 'Are you sure your reaction was pure, red-blooded rage? Not even the tiniest lacing of anything else?' she suggested, her green eyes twinkling.

Gina stared into her empty cup. 'He was a whole lot bigger than me, I know that. So I gave him a few home truths from the other side of a huge desk—and walked out.'

'Walked out? Just like that? Without giving him the brief?'

'That's exactly what I did.' She recalled the moment with some satisfaction.

'But Gina . . .' Jackie numbered several lawyers among her wide acquaintance, 'what do you do now, if you need Counsel for your client? I mean, surely none of the others in the same Chambers will take it on now, if . . .'

'No problem. I'll defend the case myself. I've done it a few times now, and there's no reason why I shouldn't. I'm quite sure,' she insisted, seeing Jackie's raised eyebrows, 'I can make as good a job of it as any inflated, prejudiced, opinionated pig of a barrister. Honestly, Jackie, he made my blood boil.'

'I can see that,' her friend observed, gazing at her quizzically. 'Well, I hope you know what you're doing. When does it come up?'

'Rather soon, actually—end of August. I advised her to stick with the Magistrates so she wouldn't have too long to wait. She could have opted to go before a jury, but Sam reckons people's chances are much the same either way in cases like this—and months of waiting around can play havoc with the nerves.'

'Hmm,' was Jackie's only comment. She changed the subject. 'How is the lovely Sam, by the way? Now, there's a really sweet man.'

'Lovely as ever. Yes, he could teach some of his fellows a thing or two. Nothing sexist about him.'

'And what about Brian?' Jackie enquired, before Gina could get carried away on another burst of outraged indignation. 'I don't seem to hear much about him these days. He's a sweet man too, you know.'

'Of course he is. He's very . . . sweet.'

'Sweet on you, too,' remarked Jackie acutely.

'Maybe.'

'Maybe, nothing. You know perfectly well he thinks you're the best thing this side of Paradise. You do like him, don't you, Gina?'

'I like him—of course I do. We work together. We get on well.'

'Is that all it is—a friendly professional relationship?' Jackie pressed.

Gina shrugged. 'You know how it is, Jackie. I'm fond of Brian, but there's no . . . you know . . .'

'Spark? Excitement?'

'No.' Gina's expression was wry. 'Not a lot of those.

We have many interests in common ... but when it comes to ...'

'To what makes things click between men and women?' suggested Jackie, sensing that her friend was having unusual difficulty finding the right words.

'If you like. There's none of that—not for me, in any case.'

'Well, judging by the way he looks at you, there is for him. Last time I saw you together—when we came round to you for dinner, wasn't it?—I was struck by the way he could hardly take his eyes off you. If you ask me, Gina, he's got it bad. I should treat him with caution, if I were you.'

'But what am I supposed to do?' Suddenly exhausted, Gina buried her face in her hands. 'First I get involved with a man with whom I share absolutely nothing but ...'

'Sexual attraction? Passion?' prompted Jackie helpfully.

'Physically,' Gina agreed, 'Pete and I were ... compatible. But otherwise it was empty—I can see that now. I was too young to see it at the time, but now I know how important it is—the companionship, the friendship—only you need more than that, too. You need both,' she declared, uncovering her face to stare at Jackie almost angrily. 'That's what it is. You need both!'

'Quite a major discovery,' commented Jackie quietly.

'Oh, I haven't only just made it. I've known it for years—but I don't believe it's possible to achieve. It doesn't exist, does it, Jackie? It's either got to be like it was with Pete—exciting at first, then ... nothing; or like it is with Brian—pleasant, safe, easy-going ...'

'And dull?'

'Well—hasn't it?'

Jackie was silent, considering the question carefully. 'I wouldn't say that, Gina,' she said at last. 'No. It's a bit like a see-saw, when you do get both things combined in one person. Sometimes one of them is uppermost, then the other. But it can work.' She paused. 'Yes,' she repeated vehemently, 'it can.'

'It works for you, doesn't it? And James?' Gina's tone was hesitant; their conversations were often direct and candid, but had rarely reached as far into the personal as this. Gina's natural reserve, and Jackie's tact, hardly ever allowed it.

'I'd say the balance was pretty good,' Jackie replied slowly. 'But it's quite a rare find in the first place, and takes a bit of hard work to maintain. It's not nearly as simple as romantic stories might have us believe,' she said firmly.

'I don't have time any more,' Gina stated, 'for romance, fictional or otherwise. The whole thing's a myth, if you ask me.'

'You've got good reason to feel like that,' Jackie reminded her gently. 'But you've still got time, Gina— you're . . . what is it . . . four years younger than me, for God's sake—not even thirty yet? You've hardly started!'

'I rather think I finished before I started,' said Gina gloomily. Then she shook herself out of a rapidly descending torpor. 'And now, I must get that little boy off your hands, and take him home. The tea and chat were just what I needed—thanks, Jackie.'

'Don't thank me, love. Seeing you at the end of the day does me almost as much good as seeing James—I keep telling you!'

Gina grinned as she stood up and stretched. 'Better not tell him that—he'll start getting jealous of me. Now, that would be a new one for the books.'

They both laughed as they went into the hall. 'Toby!' Gina called. 'Time to go home!'

'By the way, before you go,' Jackie said, sorting through a pile of coats and school bags until she found Toby's. 'Make a date for this party we're having—the one I've been making all these quiches and things for. It's going to be a big one. We've decided to start early in the evening, so we can use the garden and people can bring their kids ... I only hope it's a nice day. When I make plans like this, it always rains. James says I must be mad even to consider putting my trust in the English weather.'

'I think it's a great idea. Even if it does rain, you've got enough room to absorb quite a few people in here,' Gina reassured her.

'True—but I'd rather set my heart on having it in the garden. It's looking so nice at the moment. And you can leave the birds to do all the hoovering afterwards,' she pointed out practically.

Gina laughed. 'Who's coming?'

'That's the exciting part—I couldn't tell you. James wants to invite what sounds like hundreds of contacts, get them all over with at once—people we owe hospitality to, visiting Americans; you know. If they can bring their families too, it makes it all so much less stuffy and formal than the endless round of dinner-parties. He says he's asking Sam and Martha. They've got really friendly since you introduced them, you know—Sam and James—I think Sam's doing most of the legal work for the firm these days.'

'Yes, I believe he is,' Gina said. 'I don't have much to do with that side of things. I get landed with all the conveyancing.'

'And dealing with arrogant barristers. Anyway,' Jackie continued quickly, 'you must come. Brian'll be there too, I'm sure, if Sam's coming.'

'I expect so. I'll be there—thanks, Jackie—your parties are always great. I'll look forward to it— perhaps I can help. And do you really want Toby around?'

'Why not? He can always bed down with Joe, when the time comes for the young to make a graceful withdrawal from the scene.'

'You've got to be joking. If the time comes, more like. Let children in on social events like these, and they've got more staying-power than most of us so-called grown-ups. They'll still be rampaging about, well after midnight.'

'Such cynicism, Mrs Barton—and you such a devoted mother, too. Well, bring Toby anyway. Joe's at his most manic, surrounded by strangers, and Toby's a calming influence—I'd have asked him along, even if you weren't coming!'

'In that case,' said Gina, 'I'd better not deprive you of his company. When is this beanfeast?'

'The first Saturday in August—about three weeks' time, isn't it?' She groaned. 'School holidays will be well under way. I shall have to be thoroughly organised to be ready in time. It's quite exciting, really, though,' she said again—almost as if convincing herself, Gina thought. 'James summons all these people, and I just sit here, waiting for them to turn up.'

'You just do all the work,' Gina commented drily. 'TOBY!' she called again, up the stairs. 'Come ON—NOW!'

'I don't mind, Gina,' Jackie protested. 'I like it—really. I enjoy it.'

'I know, Jackie. Don't mind me—I'm tired, that's all. Tired, bitter and twisted.'

Jackie grinned as the two small boys hurtled down the stairs like a full force tornado. 'Not you,' she said. 'You may be tired, but there's nothing bitter about you, or twisted. You're the sweetest, straightest person I know—and don't let anyone tell you otherwise!'

Gina returned the grin. 'Thanks for the testimonial,' she said.

The next morning, Gina broke her news to Sam. 'I'm representing the client in the shoplifting case myself,' she announced, as soon as he was safely ensconced behind his chaotic desk. 'You know—the one I told you about yesterday.'

He glanced up at her sharply. 'Why on earth? Didn't you go and see this Rees character? Michele told me you were going over there—and Brian tells me he's an excellent man, with a stupendous reputation ... so what happened?'

'He's taking on all those other briefs we'd already left with John Slade. We went through them, and it was fine.'

'So?' Sam tapped on his desk with a broken pencil, frowning as he studied her. 'Why not one more? It means a lot to you, too, that one—I could tell.'

'That's just the point. It wasn't going to mean ... quite the same to him. He's not at all like John or Richard, Sam—he's a very different type.'

'Different? In what way? I mean, no Counsel is supposed to refuse a case unless they have an exceptionally strong reason.'

'Oh, he didn't refuse. He'd have done it willingly enough.'

'Then why ...?' Sam was becoming more and more bewildered.

'I wouldn't let him, that's why.' Her dark eyes flashed unusual defiance.

'You wouldn't?' He looked intrigued. 'Why ever not, Gina?'

'He was ... unsympathetic, that's all. I'd rather not go into it now, Sam.' He continued to stare searchingly at her, so she continued, reluctantly. 'We fell out over a matter of principle. He came out with the most blatantly ridiculous sexist rubbish I've had the misfortune to hear, if you really want to know. His opinions on the subject of shoplifters in general, and female ones in particular, are little short of slanderous.'

'But did you explain that the woman is not technically guilty? That her intention was not to steal?'

'Oh, I explained all right. But that just made it worse. I got the impression he'd have preferred a good, honest piece of dishonesty to ... female lack of concentration. He was extremely rude, Sam. So ...'

'So ...?'

'So there was no way I could let him defend Mrs Haines after that.'

'So . . .?' he reiterated, his bright eyes fixed on her face.

'So I shall defend her myself.'

'Are you sure you want to, Gina? You haven't had all that much experience of criminal hearings. I'll do it, if you like.'

He didn't try to press her to change her mind, she noticed; he made no value judgment, came out with no moral censure. Why couldn't all men be like him? 'I know you would, Sam,' she said warmly. 'I expect Brian would, too, if I asked him. And both of you would probably do it better than me. But I'm determined to have a go—it's a matter of pride now, if you like.'

Sam was still regarding her closely. 'I can see that your disagreement has really upset you. It's unlike you to go off at the deep end, Gina—in fact, I hardly ever remember you doing it, all the time I've known you.'

'I hardly ever do it,' she confirmed.

He leaned back in his chair, smiling. 'Well, heaven preserve me from ever being at the receiving end when you do bare your teeth, Mrs Barton. I don't envy friend Rees, if he was.'

'Mr Rees,' she informed him succinctly, 'is more than able to take care of himself. Don't waste any sympathy on him—keep your solidarity for any woman who's unfortunate enough to come into contact with him.'

'I'd better come with you, next time you go and see him—to protect you,' he suggested innocently. 'Anyway, I'm fascinated to meet this—this monster.'

'There won't be a next time, if I can help it. And I can look after myself too,' she reminded him. 'But you don't mind if I take on the case, Sam?'

'Of course not, Gina. If that's what you want to do. I'll help all I can.'

*   *   *

Later in the day, when she had a clear half-hour ahead of her, Gina was faced with the job of explaining the new turn of events to Peggy Haines herself. She got Michele to dial their home number, hoping she would be there.

'Mrs Haines? I'm glad to have caught you in. This is Gina Barton, from Goldman and Gillow.'

'Oh yes?' The woman sounded nervous, Gina thought—not surprisingly. 'I don't go out much, at ... at the moment. Is there some—news, then?'

'There won't be any news, Mrs Haines—not till the case comes up. But I'm calling to tell you there's been a slight change of plan.'

'Oh yes?' The voice quavered anxiously.

'Nothing at all to worry about. In fact, it makes it all the more simple; it's just that I've decided, if you agree, to defend you at Court myself.'

'Yourself? But is that ... I mean, are you allowed ... I mean, is it okay?'

'Of course it is, Mrs Haines. I told you the other day, solicitors do it all the time. In a higher Court you'd need a barrister—but it's part of our job too.'

'Well if you're sure ...' she still sounded doubtful.

'I'm sure—if you are. Talk to your husband about it. See what you both think. It should come cheaper this way—but that's not why I made the decision.'

'Why did you, then?'

'I just decided it wasn't worth bothering with all the fuss of getting you together with Counsel—putting you through more trauma and upheaval—when you've been through so much already,' Gina explained, crossing her fingers and hoping she'd be forgiven for this piece of invention. 'I'm perfectly capable of representing you myself, so ...'

'Well, I'm quite happy about it if you are,' Peggy said.

'Good. That's fine. We'll meet again then, before the day, and go through the whole thing once more, shall we?'

'Yes please, Mrs Barton. Tell me when, so Jim can take time off. His boss is being ever so nice—says Jim can have time off when he needs it to come with me to see you, and go to Court and that . . .' Her voice wavered still more, and Gina sensed she was close to tears.

'You must still be feeling very shocked, Mrs Haines,' she said gently. 'But don't worry—you're in good hands. We'll do everything we can.'

'Everyone's being so good.' There was a distinct crack in the voice now. 'All the family—and you—and my friends—they're all being so kind. I was ashamed at first, but people keep telling me how they've nearly done the same; how it wasn't my fault and that . . . even the doctor . . .'

'The doctor?' Gina interrupted sharply. 'Did you go and see him?'

'Her. Yes, I wanted something to help me sleep. I haven't been sleeping too well,' she explained. 'Our doctor talked to me about it. She said we all make mistakes, and I shouldn't feel bad.'

'Of course you shouldn't,' Gina soothed. 'She was quite right. No one with any . . . humanity or decency would tell you anything else. We're all on your side,' she declared emphatically, 'and anyone who isn't doesn't know what he's talking about.'

Peggy wondered, through her haze of anxiety, why that nice gentle Mrs Barton was being so unusually vehement.

CHAPTER FOUR

During the next three weeks, two of Gina's cases came up in Court; and both clients—superbly defended by Dai Rees—were acquitted. One of the verdicts had been half expected, but the other came as a pleasant surprise to all concerned—not least the defendant himself.

Gina contrived not to be present at either of the hearings. She received the news, on each occasion, from jubilant clients who came to the office afterwards. 'Wonderful man, that Mr Rees,' the second one raved. 'And all the work you put in must have helped too, Mrs Barton,' he went on quickly.

She smiled. 'As long as you're pleased, Mr Brady.'

'Pleased? I'm over the moon! I think you've all done a magnificent job. I hope you'll thank Mr Rees for me personally,' he enthused.

'We shall; but you'll be receiving your bill for his fee in due course, along with ours, I dare say,' she reminded him, a trifle drily.

'Worth every penny,' he assured her happily.

Sam was equally impressed. 'He must be good. Did you go along and listen?'

She shook her head. 'I did not. I wasn't needed, and I have other things to do with my time. But I gather my instructions did not go unheeded.'

'How did he manage it, with that Brady case? Sheer rhetoric? I didn't think there was a chance in hell.'

'A point of law, I understand. He cited a long-buried precedent—Mr Brady wasn't able to tell me which, but the law reports will doubtless divulge the details. Anyway, whatever it was, it seems to have done the trick.' She sighed heavily. 'I should have spotted it first, of course.'

'Don't underestimate yourself, Gina. Your briefings are always clear and comprehensive. If you missed this particular obscurity, it's hardly your fault. You two obviously made a better team than you thought,' he remarked, staring at a spot on the ceiling.

She pursed up her mouth. 'No comment. From now on I plan to nail down Richard Noble for my own cases. You and Brian can brief the great Dai Rees—my ambition is to avoid him.'

'There's no need to come face to face, you know, Gina,' he pointed out gently. 'Almost all of it can be done by post, or on the 'phone at the very most.'

'Not with this character. He appreciates the personal touch—he said so himself. It's partly what makes him so successful, I suspect.'

'Then I expect you'd like me to 'phone and thank him for his success on the firm's behalf?' offered Sam, with a grave twinkle.

She glanced at him gratefully. 'I would, Sam. Thank you very much.'

'I thought you might. No problem. I must admit I'm curious to know what the man's like, after all this build-up. Anyone who can get under your skin as he appears to have done—and then go on to achieve such outstanding results in Court—must be quite something.'

'I suppose you could describe him as that,' conceded Gina reluctantly.

Meanwhile life continued. Warm, close weather made office routine seem even more hectic. The school year came to an end, and Gina was more grateful than ever to Jackie when Toby spent most of his days round at her house with Joe—building dens in the long, rambling garden with its secluded wooded patch at the bottom, and generally indulging in the endlessly imaginative games that seven-year-olds invent. He had other friends too, who were more than willing to entertain him; he was a popular boy, not only with his contemporaries but with their parents as well, and everyone was glad to help out when they knew of Gina's circumstances.

In mid-August, she would drive Toby up to her parents, and leave him there with them for a fortnight in the Cotswold village where they had always lived— a treat both he and his doting grandparents eagerly looked forward to. Then she would return to join them for the last week of his holidays—a prospect that kept her going through the long, stuffy days. It would be wonderful to escape from the city; to bask for ten blissful days in the beautiful tranquillity of the place, the affectionate warmth of her parents.

The fates smiled on Jackie. The morning of her party dawned bright and fine. Gina spent the whole day there, mucking in with preparations for the evening. Jackie was admirably organised, of course: stacks of mouth-watering food had been taken out of the deep freeze to thaw; plentiful supplies of drink were lined up ready for the onslaught. But there was the house to prepare too, and Gina donned her scruffiest jeans and a headscarf, rolled up the sleeves of her oldest loose top, and buckled to with a will. It was the least she could do after all Jackie's help; and anyway, she enjoyed it.

James—darkly good-looking in jeans and shirt-sleeves—supervised operations in the garden, while Jackie issued instructions indoors. Gina was one of a small army of volunteers—colleagues and friends— who had dropped in to lend a hand with shifting rugs and furniture, and generally heaving things about. Two of them were busy assisting James with the electrics: there was wiring to be done, so that speakers could carry music to each room as well as to the garden. Then there were fairy-lights to be strung from trees and bushes, and coloured spotlamps to be rigged up near the house, so that the scene after sunset would be suitably magical. Trestle tables were opened on the patio above the lawn, ready to be loaded with some of the delicious products of Jackie's days of baking.

At five o'clock, Gina and Toby retreated down the road to get themselves ready; and two hours later—as the sultry afternoon gave way to a soft, balmy evening—they were reporting back, almost unrecognisably transformed (in Gina's case, at least) into festive party guests. After a long, relaxing soak in a scented bath, she had chosen her favourite summer dress—full and floating, flattering her fine curves with its soft lines and dainty bootlace shoulder-straps; setting off her smooth, naturally olive skin and her honey-brown eyes with its glowing sun-gold tones. She had coiled her richly shining hair lower and more loosely than usual, and wore only her customary simple gold jewellery: two thin bangles, the wedding ring, the tiny, delicate chain round her neck. Bare legs, yellow canvas espadrilles laced up her slim ankles, a touch of musky perfume at her throat—and she was ready for anything.

Toby had suffered himself to be scrubbed free of the day's accumulated grime; and had succumbed without struggle to a fresh pair of jeans and a clean tee-shirt, his fair curls neatly brushed into a rare semblance of order. Within ten minutes, as Gina was fully aware, he would be the untidy urchin he had been two hours ago—but at least he had shown willing.

Jackie greeted them at the door, a picture herself in a black-and-green cotton trouser suit. 'Good lord—don't you both look smart—what a transmogrification! Joe's in the garden, Toby, getting in everyone's way—and Ben's around somewhere—and there are several other children arriving. Sam and Martha should be here soon, with their girls . . .'

Toby succeeded in conveying, by the merest twitch of an eyebrow, his opinion of Sam and Martha's girls; but he was much too polite to put it into words. 'I'll go and find Joe, then,' he said instead, treating them to his most winning smile; then he disappeared through french windows which stood invitingly open on to lush lawns and bright borders.

Gina gazed with satisfaction at the scene, both inside and out. 'It's all ... perfect, Jackie. It looks lovely—and so do you. You've worked so hard, I do hope you enjoy your party. You deserve to.'

'I intend to,' the other woman declared, sounding as if she meant it. 'And I'm not the only one who's worked hard, Gina. You've been at it all day too. I don't know how you manage to come back so fresh and beautiful after all that heavy labour—I was so grateful.'

'Don't be silly,' it was Gina's turn to protest. 'I really enjoy doing things like that for a change. It's good for me, after sitting around all week, using my grey cells and not a lot else.'

'Well, tonight's a night for giving your brain a rest and letting your physical self take over. Have a few drinks—try some of my special quiches and salads—let yourself go. You never know,' she leaned conspiratorially closer, 'there might be a wonderfully eligible bachelor among these mystery guests James has invited.' She giggled. 'I still don't know who half of them are. He did give me a list, but I've had such a lot to think about ... most of them are his cronies in advertising, and there's a contingent of visiting Swedes ... and Sam, of course, and Brian ... when's he coming, by the way? Did he say?'

Gina didn't bother to interrupt her hostess's excited flow of chatter in order to point out, for the umpteenth time, that she was not on the look-out for bachelors, eligible or otherwise. 'He'll be along soon, I expect,' she replied. 'He's usually punctilious about time. You said seven-thirty, didn't you?'

'We did.'

'Then I'm sure that's when he'll arrive,' Gina said.

At seven-thirty, on the dot, Brian appeared at the french windows. The party atmosphere was coming to life as more cars rolled up outside and more guests piled into the house and out into the garden— laughing, chatting, helping themselves to refreshments, standing in groups or strolling on the grass. Jackie was in her element, circulating among them, welcoming everyone—friends and strangers alike—with equally charming warmth. James, suave now in a light tan suit, did the honours, handing out drinks as he introduced his various contacts to one another.

Brian, dressed as always in a conventional grey suit and white shirt, gazed round the throng until his eyes lit on Gina; then he made straight for her. She was well into her third glass of wine, and already feeling more than a touch light-headed.

'Hallo Gina. You look ... very nice.' The look in his eyes told her he would like to say more; but compliments did not come easy to Brian.

'Hallo, Brian. Have a drink. Lovely evening, isn't it? Lovely party?' She beamed at him, more meltingly than usual.

He stared at her. 'Lovely. How many of those have you had?'

She counted; then she counted again. 'Only two, before this one. I don't often indulge, you know,' she pointed out defensively. 'And I haven't eaten yet, so I suppose it seems like more. But I don't have to drive home, so I thought ... just this once. It was Jackie who suggested it,' she explained vaguely.

He smiled. 'This isn't a prosecution, Mrs Barton. You deserve your relaxation as much as anyone. Especially after recent successes.'

'Successes?' She frowned.

'In Court. I haven't congratulated you on them yet.'

'Oh, those. I had nothing to do with those, as you well know. That was all down to the charismatic Mr Dai Rees. I wasn't even there.'

'Nonetheless, you put in the spadework; and two out of two is an achievement,' he insisted. 'I haven't met this Rees yet. What's he like?'

'Tall, dark and arrogant,' she informed him without hesitation. 'You haven't missed a thing.'

'I did hear,' began Brian cautiously, 'that you fell

out over one of your cases, and decided to take it on
yourself?'

She regarded him levelly. 'Sam's told you, has he?
Yes, well—I'd rather not go into it now, Brian, if you
don't mind; but that's about the size of it, yes.'

'When does it come up?' he pressed, a little
anxiously.

'Soon. Now, if you don't mind,' she repeated
firmly, 'I'm here to enjoy myself tonight; so let's not
talk shop.'

'Okay.' Brian glanced at her, again with that edge of
uncertainty. Then he shrugged. 'I'll go and find a
drink. Want another one?' he offered doubtfully,
looking at her empty glass.

Gina looked at it too. 'Why not? As I said—I
haven't got far to walk home. Dry white wine, please
Brian.'

'I'll be back in a minute,' he promised.

'You do that,' she said—wishing the thought made
her feel more enthusiastic.

Daylight was rapidly fading into the subtle tones of
dusk, and James's fairy-lit setting was coming into its
own. Music filtered through the strategically-placed
speakers—atmospheric but not intrusive. Laughter
and conversation echoed from every corner; children
ran about, squealing and fighting as children will—
tolerated by most adults, ignored by a few. Gina felt
content to wander on her own among the trees and
bushes which had been so carefully planted, years ago,
at the far end of this beautifully-matured garden—
giving an impression of a small country estate rather
than an urban residence at the heart of a great city.
There was a sense of peace in being alone for a few
minutes—alone, and yet part of a happy crowd.

A cluster of people stood quite near her now, talking
animatedly. Her attention was caught by some familiar
words which strayed towards her across the still air:
legal terms, *tort* and *injunction* and *inchoate* and
defamation. Lawyers—was there no escaping them?

Not wishing to get involved on this evening off, she turned away; but then she recognised one of the voices, and turned back.

It was Sam, of course—always at the centre, sociable, vociferous; and next to him was Martha, who had been a Legal Executive before their marriage and who knew as much about the subject as he did. Beside her stood James, who was pretty well-informed on most matters; and then ... whose was the broad back, the unruly black hair—the presence, standing out from the rest of them ... head and shoulders above Sam, and half a head even above James, who was not a short man? Close to him—one arm possessively linked in his, her svelte form nestling up to him seductively—stood a *soignée* blonde whom Gina did not recognise.

But she recognised the man all right, and as soon as he spoke she was in no doubt at all. That deep timbre, the lilting Welsh tune to the words—they touched an answering chord somewhere inside her, causing pulses to race, her stomach to churn. What the hell was Dai Rees doing here, at Jackie's party? Had Sam brought him? Perhaps he knew James, who had friends in just about every corner of London life? And who was the elegant blonde beside him? His wife? His lady friend? It was no business of Gina's—but curiosity swept over her in a strangely sickening wave, and she backed away—half-afraid of finding out, more than half-afraid to face him.

So far, she was safe: they were all too intent on their own discussions to notice her. Sam was holding forth as usual, and Martha was adding her own embellishments to the story. Dai Rees had his back turned squarely to Gina and was hardly likely to swing round suddenly if she kept quiet. She moved further away from them, melting into the welcome dimness among the trees, becoming as inconspicuous as possible.

She couldn't evade Brian that way, though. By the time he returned, bearing two glasses, the little group had dispersed and disappeared. Gina was alone again—her heart thumping a little (perhaps with relief?), but outwardly collected. 'What on earth are you doing, down here in the gloom?' he demanded. 'I thought I'd lost you.'

'No, Brian.' She took a fortifying sip of wine. 'You haven't lost me. I'm still here. I just don't seem to be feeling very . . . social.'

He took a step nearer to peer into her face. 'Are you all right, Gina? Is there anything wrong?'

She hoped her smile was reassuring. 'Absolutely fine thanks, Brian. Maybe I've just had a bit too much to drink, all at once, on an empty stomach.'

'Maybe you have,' Brian agreed heavily. His arm had crept around her waist in an uncharacteristically bold gesture. She tried to steel herself against it—not to flinch from his touch, fearing to offend him. 'Gina . . .' his voice was hoarse. 'I'd hate you to be unhappy—you know that, don't you? I'm . . . I'm awfully fond of you, you know. I . . .'

Such declarations were not Brian's normal style. Gina glanced round, almost hoping now for an interruption—wondering how she was going to nip this potentially difficult moment in the bud. Her prayer was answered in the shape of a tall, burly figure which loomed unexpectedly up at them out of the dusk.

For a split second she froze: the remedy, in this case, might just be worse than the ailment. But it was too late for escape this time. Those sharp grey eyes had spotted her; that powerful voice was already greeting her as he approached.

'Mrs Barton, isn't it? What a pleasant surprise! I did wonder, when I was introduced to the Goldmans, whether I might also find you here—but even so, an old cliché might be in order—something about a small world—don't you think?'

Her tongue was momentarily paralysed, her senses peculiarly overwhelmed by his proximity. No man had the right to carry such a potent effect about with him.

Making a determined effort, she fought it off. 'Mr Rees—may I introduce . . .?'

Brian stood, his arm still around her, his pale blue eyes fixed on the intruder. Dai Rees nodded affably in his direction and interrupted before Gina could go any further: 'You must be Mr Barton? The fortunate man who lays claim to this . . . spirited young lady?'

Gina's hackles rose at the mockery in his tone; she lifted her head to return his direct, insolent gaze. 'I should hardly think one person could . . . *lay claim to* another, Mr Rees. As I was saying, may I introduce my friend and senior partner, Brian Gillow. Brian— Mr Dai Rees.'

Brian removed his right hand from Gina's waist and held it out to the other man, his face a study in embarrassment. Eventually he found his voice. 'Good evening, Mr Rees. I've—I've heard a lot about you, of course; but I—I didn't expect to meet you here.'

'The pleasure and the surprise are both mutual, I assure you.' Dai shook the offered hand warmly, his eyes now summing Brian up with undisguised curiosity. 'I do beg your pardon for the case of mistaken identity, Mr Gillow. I really did put my foot in my big mouth this time, it seems. Jumped to all the wrong conclusions,' he added, with a glance which remarked: *and you can hardly blame me.* 'Please forgive me.' Despite the apologetic words he was perfectly relaxed, his poise totally unruffled. 'Naturally, seeing you together, I assumed you to be . . . together.'

Gina cringed from the smooth tone, the eyes which spoke volumes; but she faced him out. 'Mr Gillow and I are old friends,' she told him calmly.

'We—er—have plenty to talk about,' Brian explained lamely. He shifted from one foot to the other, uncertain whether or not to enlighten Dai Rees on the matter of Gina's real marital status—and decided it was best left to her. She could be so touchy about her private life, he knew. He changed the subject as fast as possible. 'I must add mine to the general congratulations. We were all delighted with the outcome of those cases you defended.'

Dai bowed slightly to acknowledge the praise, accepting it gracefully. 'How kind of you, Mr Gillow. It was most stimulating, being briefed by Mrs Barton. I'm sure that was a factor behind my success.' His words could hardly be faulted, but something underlay them which was definitely insulting.

Brian swallowed hard, causing his rather prominent Adam's apple to move visibly. 'Are you a friend of James and Jackie, Mr Rees? Or have you come with Sam?'

'Neither. I have only just had the pleasure of meeting the Goldmans. I was brought along by a colleague of James's ... being a relative newcomer to London and obviously in need of care and protection in being launched on the metropolitan scene.'

Gina suppressed a smile: no one could be less in need of care or protection than Dai Rees. Glancing at him, she received a sardonic grin in return.

'Which colleague was that?' Brian was asking, relieved to have got off personal matters. 'Perhaps I know him?'

'Not a him—a her,' Dai Rees elucidated. 'Perhaps you do—Miss Linda Green. We are near neighbours in the same apartment block in Primrose Hill. She has been kind enough to take a ... neighbourly interest in me, lonely bachelor as I am. She suggested that I might like to accompany her this evening, and I accepted—having no other engagements, and being happy to meet her friends. I'm doubly glad now,' he concluded politely, 'that I did.'

'Linda Green. No, I don't think I know her. Do you, Gina?' Brian enquired, relaxing now as the alcohol took its loosening effect.

'No,' replied Gina succinctly.

'Well,' Brian went on, eager in his determination to cover the earlier awkward moment, 'I've been hoping for the opportunity to meet you. Gina was just talking about you, as a matter of fact.'

The penetrating gaze swivelled in her direction. 'Was she now? Nothing incriminating, I hope?'

Gina hoped her blush was camouflaged in the dim light. 'Not at all,' Brian protested—far too quickly. 'We were just saying how impressed we were by your performance.' Suddenly in need of more Dutch courage, he drained his glass. 'I need a refill.' There was a touch of desperation in his tone. 'Can I get you another, Mr Rees?'

'Not for me, thanks, Mr Gillow. And do call me Dai. These formalities are so Anglo-Saxon and archaic, don't you think?'

'Fair enough—Dai. I'm Brian, then.' He turned to Gina. 'Gina? More wine?'

She thought fast. She didn't want another drink; but the last thing she did want was to be left alone here with Dai Rees. 'I think I could do with some food,' she decided.

'Good idea,' Dai said at once. 'Allow me to accompany you. I could use some myself.' Gina's heart sank, but she turned in silence to walk back to the house.

'I'll see you both over there.' Brian set off ahead of them at a purposeful trot, clutching his empty glass as if it was a lifeline, obviously glad of the chance to escape. *A fine friend he is in times of challenge*, Gina's mind taunted irritatingly, as she walked beside Dai across the spotlit patio.

They were accosted, near the french windows, by two hurtling, swooping miniature highwaymen. 'There you are, Toby!' Gina seized the diversion thankfully. 'I was wondering where you'd got to. I hope you haven't been a nuisance?'

'Of course we haven't.' Tony glared at her, distinctly pained.

'We've been playing Murder,' Joe announced lugubriously. 'We've killed sixteen people—so far.'

'I didn't realise it was going to be that kind of party,' drawled Dai Rees, grinning down at them, 'or

I'd have brought my six-shooter.' Then he crouched to their level and studied their faces. 'Unless I'm very much mistaken, this young man belongs to our charming hostess. With this colouring, he has to.'

'I don't *belong* to anyone,' growled Joe. 'I'm Joe. Jackie's my mum, and James is my dad.'

Gina looked away to hide her amusement; but Dai nodded solemnly, accepting the reproof. 'You're quite right, Joe. People don't belong to each other—I don't know what made me use the word.' He turned to Toby, who had moved closer to Gina and was surveying the stranger in silence. 'And I bet you're Gina's son, aren't you? You must be, with those eyes ... but your father must be fair. Am I right?' His own eyes searched the crowded garden, as if hoping to locate the man himself.

There was a strange sense of triumph—almost of elation—in the way Gina's heart raced at his words. So, even Dai Rees could be 'right' once too often. Her hand rested protectively on Toby's shoulder, in case he had been hurt by the ignorant, unintentional barb.

Joe, who had no such sensitivities on his friend's behalf, came to the rescue. 'Toby hasn't got a father,' he pointed out in disparaging tones which suggested that everyone, surely, knew *that*? 'Have you, Tobe? He's only got Gina.'

There was a second's poignant silence; but Dai Rees was not a man to be disconcerted for long. Standing up to face Gina, his expression now completely sincere, he said simply: 'I apologise again, Mrs Barton. I had no idea—not the least idea.' Then he bent down again to speak directly to Toby, his dark head close to the boy's fair one. 'Toby, I'm very sorry if I've said anything to hurt you. I only know your mother a little, and I didn't realise. No one told me.' There was an edge of reproach in the glance he flicked up at Gina, but his tone was extraordinarily gentle as he spoke to her son.

Toby's face lit up in a broad smile. 'It doesn't

matter. You didn't know. I don't need a dad, anyway,'
he added proudly. 'I've got my mum, haven't I?'

Gina turned away again, this time swallowing the
lump in her throat. 'Yes, Toby,' she only half heard
Dai say, 'that's very true. And I expect she's worth a
hundred dads put together.'

She glanced sharply at him after this odd remark;
but he was still looking at Toby. Joe was growing
bored of this conversation. 'Let's get on with our
game, Tobe. There's some girls over there we haven't
marked out yet. They should be exterminated.' He
lingered over the word with evident relish. 'And,' he
told his friend importantly, 'there's a whole bowl of
crisps in the kitchen they've forgotten to bring in, and
I know where they are, so if you come I'll show you.'

Toby hesitated, but Gina gave him a little push and
he ran off after Joe—sending her a bright smile over
his shoulder as he went. 'See you later,' she called.

This time the silence seemed to go on for hours.
Looking down at her feet, Gina was acutely aware of
Dai's penetrating gaze upon her. Eventually, he spoke.
'I seem destined to ... trample on your sensitive
points, Mrs Barton. Once again, I must apologise for a
positive series of *faux pas* this evening. You keep your
private self so—private...' he observed, his eyes
narrowing as he scrutinised her. Again, she detected
that air of reproof in his tone.

'I make a point of keeping it private. As Toby said,
you weren't to know. After all,' she reminded him
blandly, 'we've only met once.'

'Have we really?' The dark brows lifted. 'Strange—
it seems I've known you longer than that.' She said
nothing; but something in her mind echoed his words.
'It's surprising,' he went on, 'that I haven't picked up
anything about your ... situation from other people in
the trade. You know how they gossip—but I've heard
nothing from anyone. You have loyal colleagues,
Gina.'

Her first name fell from his lips naturally. She let it

pass, just for once; she wasn't in the mood for a struggle—not tonight. 'Not all that many people do know, actually. I try not to mix my domestic affairs with my professional life.'

'I suppose all this might help to explain your rather ... overheated reaction to my remarks the other week,' he speculated, gazing at her thoughtfully.

'I hardly think so,' she retorted at once. 'Nor do I think they were overheated. Please don't go away with the notion that your success with our other cases has caused me to change my opinion of your comments on that occasion.'

'I certainly won't.' The carved features broke into a grin. 'Shall we go and find this food, or has my tactlessness driven your appetite away?'

'It takes far more than that,' she told him defiantly, 'to diminish my appetite.'

'I'm glad to hear it. Let's go and see what's left, then, before all these kids demolish the lot.' He was social, conversational—she found it difficult, keeping up with his shifts of mood.

They strolled into the house together. A few acquaintances nodded and smiled at Gina, casting inquisitive glances towards her unknown companion. In the distance she could see Jackie, pink and bubbling, busily making her guests feel at home. Dai appeared to be following her thoughts.

'Lovely lady, our hostess, isn't she?' he observed. 'A good friend of yours?' They had reached the table and stood admiring the lavish spread of dishes.

'Oh yes, very.' Gina helped herself to a piece of succulent tandoori chicken, nestling temptingly on its bed of salad, the meat glazed a beautiful dark red. Then she spooned out some savoury rice to go with it. 'Joe and Toby have been at school together ever since the nursery class.'

'So,' he guessed, as they carried their loaded plates out into the garden again, by unspoken agreement, 'you're a resident of Camden Town too?'

'I live about ten houses away.'

'Nice area to live in, isn't it? I don't live far away myself.'

'So you said—Primrose Hill.' Near (or with?) the glamorous Miss Green.

'With the park,' he continued, 'and central London on the doorstep, and all these fascinating shops.'

'It's the most cosmopolitan part of London, I often think,' she said, pausing to pick up her piece of chicken and bite a small chunk from it. He was surprisingly easy to talk to—particularly if you were careful to stick to trivial things.

'And quite handy for King's Cross,' he commented. 'Do you drive to work every day?'

'Most days. Parking can be a problem, unless I arrive very early. I hate all that rushing out to feed meters or move the car. In a way I prefer to use the Tube.'

'I hate the things. Hot and claustrophobic.' He shuddered.

Gina glanced at him as they walked on again. So, even he had his little weaknesses—and, more surprisingly, admitted to them. A disconcerting, contradictory man. 'Don't you drive, then?'

'Good God, yes. Been behind the wheel since I was a teenager. Wouldn't be without a car.' Gina could imagine the kind of car it would be, too: fast, smooth, expensive—showy.

Almost before she had realised it, they had meandered back to the far end of the garden—perhaps following a mutual instinct to head for the spaces away from other people. Suddenly panicky, Gina looked around, wondering where Brian had vanished to. There was something dangerously attractive about being alone—or effectively alone—with Dai Rees in the moonlit thicket at the bottom of Jackie's garden. Just for once, she hoped Brian's familiar form would hove into sight, breaking the fast-falling spell.

'Don't worry, Gina.' He was at it again, stepping

inside her head. 'I expect he's been waylaid. I'm sure he won't desert you for long—especially not leaving you to my tender mercies,' he added cynically.

So, those shrewd eyes hadn't missed the brief, intimate exchange he had stumbled upon earlier. 'I hardly need Brian to take care of me, Mr Rees,' she assured him crisply. 'I've already told you—we're simply colleagues—that's all.'

'If you say so.' His scepticism was tangible, but he refrained from voicing it. 'Are you going to stay on your high horse forever, Gina? Is there no way I can persuade you to call me Dai? Everyone else does.'

He had stopped, and turned to face her. Delicately, playing for time, she took a forkful of salad. 'All right; Dai.' She picked up the chicken leg and nibbled the last of the meat from it, eyeing him cautiously as she did so.

He watched her with amused approval. 'I like to see a woman enjoying her food. Good isn't it, this chicken?'

'One of Jackie's specialities,' she explained, licking the spicy red paprika from her fingers. 'She's a great cook.'

'A domestic soul—not a career girl like you?' he hazarded.

'She doesn't need to be,' Gina snapped, surprising herself.

'Are you a career girl because you need to be, Gina?' he replied softly. 'Or because you want to be?'

'Because I want to be, of course. I've always been one—even when . . .'

'When you lived with Toby's father?' His tone was controlled, gentle; but his eyes were sharp. 'What happened, Gina? You have such a lovely son; he must have had a father once. Obviously something went wrong?'

She stared at him, unprepared for this attack on her privacy by a relative stranger. The strong features were all attention and concentration; but was his interest personal, or was he just being the professional interviewer—the interrogator—acting out his instinct to find out how people tick?

She shrugged: perhaps it didn't really matter, either way. 'I married very young. He was an artist. He left me. That's all.'

'Left you? That's *all*?' he echoed—his tone outraged, even appalled. But Gina was unmoved: she'd heard it all before. 'Just left you—or left you for someone else?'

'Both. It was over by then anyway. I realised later it—it was bound to happen eventually.' She was carefully cool, detached.

'And are you still in touch?' he persisted. 'Does he see Toby?'

She hesitated. This was treading on dangerous territory—threatening her last and most important defence. She glanced down at her wedding ring, aware that he was doing the same. 'No.' She drew in a deep breath. 'No,' she repeated, more firmly. 'I haven't heard from him since the day he went.'

He gazed at her for a moment; then he reached out to take the empty plate from her hands and put it on the ground next to his own. He was informal tonight— short-sleeved blue cotton shirt open at the neck to show a brown chest, curling black hairs—but still, she had to admit, imposing. He leaned back against a plane tree, hands in the pockets of his casual cord trousers. 'Then why,' he murmured, his eyes fixed on hers, 'the wedding ring? The heavy emphasis on the *Mrs*? The *noli me tangere* attitude?' When she failed to answer, he supplied his own. 'Such elaborate defence mechanisms, Gina.' His voice vibrated with a low intensity.

There was a pause, during which she studied a patch of daisies—a faint white cloud in the shadowy grass—and he studied her. Then, when she still didn't reply, he went on: 'It seems I was more accurate than I could have understood, when I described you as a

Madonna. There's even more of the Virgin Mother about you than I realised.'

She raised her head at that. 'Not exactly,' she pointed out drily.

'But that was a long time ago, Gina. How many years have you been . . . on your own? Three? Four? Busy divorcée that you are—with the responsibilities of mother and father thrust on you at once—you can't have had much time for . . . personal involvements of other kinds?' he suggested, his eyes gleaming. 'Nor perhaps, after your experience, much inclination?'

She struggled hopelessly against a storm of reaction to his words and his tone. Suddenly she gave in, pushed over the edge. 'That's none of your business,' she flared—terrified to let him know how close to the truth his probing had come. 'I don't know what makes you think you have the right to interest yourself in my private life; but as it happens, I am not divorced. My official status is, I believe, described as separated.' She subsided slightly before adding, 'And I'm not in the habit of losing my temper with total strangers, Mr Rees.' She glared at him, eyes blazing. 'But you really have the knack of getting my blood up.'

He stepped round behind his tree, holding both hands in front of his face in mock self-defence. 'All right, all right, lady—I'm sorry if I touched yet another soft spot. Like I said, Mrs Barton, I seem doomed to tread on your dainty toes.' His gaze had become keen, quizzical. 'And since you mentioned blood, Gina—I was wondering—you're not a fellow-Celt, by any chance, are you? Sometimes that leads to a certain friction—we hot-blooded outlanders can usually be relied on to get one another going . . .'

She turned and walked a few steps away from him, deeper into the rustling, leafy darkness—wondering why she didn't just walk the other way, back to the people and the lights, while she had the chance. Some strange, hypnotic fascination held her there; even the anger he provoked wasn't exactly unpleasant. The whole exchange felt unreal—and yet acutely real, in a way she wasn't used to.

She stopped beside a chestnut—young and straight—and reached out a hand to touch its bark—grateful for its reassuring roughness, its hard strength against her skin. 'No,' she told him. 'As far as I know, I've got no Celtic blood at all.'

He was following her; a twig cracked sharply beneath his foot and she jumped imperceptibly. The warm, sweet-smelling night air closed around them. Under water, she thought inconsequentially—it was like being under water: green and gloomy, with moving shadows, indefinable shapes.

'Well, you're not entirely Anglo-Saxon,' he insisted. 'Not with that temper.'

'My mother's Italian,' she admitted—as if it was any concern of his.

'Aha.' He grinned—teeth a flash of white in his darkly shaded face. 'That explains your lovely name, of course. I knew there was something about you—not Celt, but Latin. It's the Latin blood talking!'

'If you say so.' She turned to face him. 'Actually, my mother is quite a placid person.'

'So are you, Gina,' he reminded her softly, 'on the outside. But inwardly—you're often seething, aren't you?' She backed up against the tree, her arms reaching round it, taking support from its solidity. 'And your father?'

'English, through and through. Comes from an old Warwickshire family. He's a Professor of Languages, in the Midlands,' she told him, with some pride.

'An unusual mixture.' He had moved in very close; now he leaned one large hand nonchalantly against her tree, just above her right shoulder. 'Does your mother come from an academic tradition as well?'

'Oh no.' She shook her head, smiling slightly. 'Her parents own a cheese factory in Lower Lombardy.'

'Now, that's a really important job, making cheese.' She glanced at him; but he appeared to be completely serious. 'I love cheese,' he confided. 'It's a major part of gastronomic life as far as I'm concerned. Do they still do it themselves—your grandparents?'

She gazed straight at him. 'You ask a lot of questions, Dai Rees.'

'When I'm interested in a person,' he returned, quietly, 'I want to know all about them.'

She cleared her throat. 'My grandparents,' she informed him, 'are alive and well and supervising the running of the firm—but I have two uncles who actually manage the factory now.'

'Have you been there yourself?' he wanted to know.

'Oh yes.' Her gaze fixed itself far away. 'When I was a child, we went every year, but since . . . I've only been once since I grew up. It's a wonderful place,' she mused, remembering it. 'I'm going to take Toby to meet them, before they die.' There was regret in her voice, and a kind of determination.

'Of course you will.' His hand was just touching her bare shoulder—giving her a strong sensation of being pinned to the trunk of the tree. 'How did they meet—your parents?'

'My father was studying Italian over there. My mother was at the same college. He brought her back, and they've been together ever since.'

'A romantic tale,' he remarked. 'Well, at least you've got one successful example of marriage before you, Gina. You know it can be done.' Was she imagining it, or was there a trace of bitterness under the words? Before she could decide, he moved still closer—dispersing such coherent thought as she had left.

All her senses were stirred by him; she felt dazed, mesmerised. It would be so easy just to duck under that muscular arm, run away into the safety of the crowd—but she didn't. She just stood there, clutching her tree, curiously helpless—she, who was never helpless in any situation. And even as she warned herself to flee from this confrontation, something in her seemed to welcome it.

'I'm no romantic, Dai. I've been cured of that—if I
ever was one.'

'I can understand that now, Gina. It can't have been
easy for you on your own.'

Warning bells rang and got louder; and then
receded into the distance as his grey eyes came into
sharp focus, just in front of hers, blurring again as
they moved in even closer. She held her breath: his
lips were feather-light against hers, as she had known
they would be; his tongue just sampling, tasting the
sweet softness of her mouth before he drew away—
lingeringly, reluctantly. It was a hint, a promise; the
secret stamping of a seal. He made no attempt to take
it any further, but Gina understood the clear message:
that one day, when the time and place were right, he
fully intended to complete what he had started.

She shivered—and managed, at last, to tear herself
out of the mysterious magnetic field which had
surrounded them. Pushing his arm away with her
hand, she abandoned the safety of her tree, taking a
step backwards in the direction of the house—the
people—reality. 'Must get back to the party,' she was
muttering feverishly, foolishly, 'see what Toby's up
to—help Jackie—find Brian . . .'

'Gina . . . Gina . . .' The fingers of both his hands
wound themselves firmly round the smooth skin of her
upper arms. 'There's nothing to be afraid of. I won't
eat you. Little Red Riding Hood doesn't have to run
out of the wood,' he added sardonically. 'The Big Bad
Wolf is quite happy to let her go free!'

It wasn't the big bad wolf she was worried about,
Gina's mind shouted hopelessly: it was herself. Her own
responses; her own needs and emotions, which had been
kept in cold storage far too long—and were now busily
making their presence felt—uncurling themselves
meaningfully in their deep dark hiding places. The
anger this man had generated on their first meeting was
intimately linked, she sensed, with other passions . . .
passions which were infinitely more threatening.

Shaking a little with shocked reaction, she set off across the lawn. Leaving the shelter of the trees, the enclosing darkness, she blinked; but she held her head high, and on the surface she was as cool as ever. He soon caught up, but—aware of curious glances around them—he kept his distance and did not touch her. Even from three feet away, his physical presence seemed to reach out and draw her towards it.

He had become all light-hearted banter again. 'Well Gina—are you still going to hold out against my professional services and refuse to let me represent your unfortunate shoplifting client? Am I still in disgrace?'

She refused to look at him. 'Presumably you haven't undergone a miraculous conversion on the subject of shoplifters, and female ones in particular?'

'Nothing has happened to change my opinions,' he assured her firmly. 'And I don't suppose it ever will. But I repeat—the offer stands. I'd do my best as I did in your other two cases.' *Which I won*, his tone reminded her; but even he was too modest to spell it out.

Gina considered, just for a moment. A shout from across the garden drew their attention to Brian, waving furiously as he loped towards them. She stopped in her tracks, turning to face her companion. 'No, Dai,' she said—quietly, quickly, confidently. 'I've told Mrs Haines I'm defending her myself. As long as your mind isn't open to change—well, neither is mine.'

His expression was wry as he studied her. 'Just as you say, Mrs Barton.'

Brian was approaching fast, red-faced and panting. 'Wherever did you get to? I went back down there again, and I couldn't see you. I went back to the house, and you weren't there either.'

'We must have missed each other on the way back, Brian,' suggested Gina sweetly.

He regarded them both reproachfully. Gina felt

irritated by the suspicion in his eyes—he was a good deal too proprietorial for her liking. 'I've been helping Jackie in the kitchen,' he said, in a tone which clearly suggested that was Gina's job. 'She says she thinks the boys should be getting to bed. Could you come and see to Toby?'

Dai stepped back—as if handing her over to the other man. 'Sorry to keep you from your maternal duties, Gina.' The grey eyes flashed humour, but the mouth was steady, impassive. 'Good to have seen you again—and to have met you, Brian. I must be pushing on—we have another party to look in on, I believe—if I can find the lovely Ms Green . . .' His cool gaze ranged over the festive scene.

'I saw her indoors, dancing,' Brian told him.

'Right. I'll go and scoop her up, then. Goodbye, Brian. Gina.' He shook hands with them, each in turn—a simple interaction between colleagues. 'I'm sure we'll meet again, in the course of duty.'

With that he swung round on his heel and marched briskly off into the sybaritic throng.

CHAPTER FIVE

GINA missed Toby. It made life simpler in some ways, of course, not having him around for a while: it meant she could go out freely without having to bother fixing up babysitters—catch up on some of the social and cultural activities she normally had so little time for. Brian was only too happy to oblige with his company at theatres, cinemas and concerts, as soon as he realised she was open to offers; and she enjoyed paying visits to friends whom she hardly ever got round to seeing.

But the flat was unnaturally empty and quiet without Toby. It wasn't that he was a particularly noisy child, but his presence radiated a special vibrancy. In his absence, Gina was always aware that a major part of her was missing—a physical piece, almost, like an amputation.

It was probably good for them both, she philosophised as she sat in the train back to London after leaving him in Gloucester. They had decided to add to his treat by making the journey by rail for a change. Toby was a railway fanatic; and it saved Gina the strain of two drives in a short time. So she had bought herself a cheap day return ticket, and Toby a single, and they had both shared in his excitement at the trip. Gina's parents had driven in to meet them at the station, and they had all gone for a happy lunch at a pizza bar before Gina had reluctantly caught her train home.

Yes, maybe they were too mutually dependent, she mused as she gazed out at the gold-and-green, high summer countryside; thrown together as they were, just the two of them. Maybe the odd break was just as well. And he'd be all right with his grandparents— more than all right—she could be sure of that.

The fact that they were in the throes of a heatwave didn't make it any easier. Sweating her way through endlessly oppressive days, she could hardly prevent her thoughts turning wistfully to the three of them—her favourite people—up there in the gloriously gentle Cotswold scenery, making the most of the weather. Shutting her eyes, she could envisage the mellow-grey stone of the village itself, glowing warm and venerable under that English sun; smell the air, so soft and clean—so far away from this metropolitan dust, and yet actually only a matter of a hundred miles or so.

She sighed, forcing herself to concentrate on the work in hand. Not long now before she could join them; meanwhile she must be strong-minded and get through more than ever to earn her holiday.

Before she could escape, there was a high hurdle to be faced: Peggy Haines's hearing. Gina tried to convince herself she was feeling perfectly calm about that; but as the day approached she knew full well it was self-delusion. She couldn't ignore the tightening tension in the pit of her stomach—the insidious sensation of foreboding. It would hardly be the first time she'd stood up in Court, of course—though she'd never, as Sam had pointed out, represented anyone in very significant or difficult criminal cases. So far, she'd always managed to remain objective. To a professional lawyer, winning or losing have to be mere technicalities; there was too much at stake, she reminded herself, for her to become personally involved.

But whether she liked it or not, she had to admit, she *was* personally involved. The outcome of this particular case had got itself confused, somewhere along the line, with her own life. Its importance had grown out of all proportion. Its challenge was at a personal, rather than a professional, level.

And if that challenge had a clear connection with Dai Rees, Gina pushed it—desperately and repeatedly—to the back of her mind. It wasn't inclined to stay there. Over and over again, her mental tape-recorder played through that first scene—how he had got her all stirred up with rage, goading her into the grim determination she now felt to tackle the case herself.

Even worse, there were those moments at Jackie's party—she could hardly bear to recall them, and yet they were with her all the time. The man had taken full advantage of the relaxed, heady atmosphere . . . he had awakened some long-submerged impulses in her, coaxed some secret responses from her . . . and now she was sick with shame.

She tossed and turned through the stifling city nights, accusing herself, blaming him, never quite sure where the target of her fury actually lay. She buried hot cheeks in her pillows. She had to face it: to him, it must have seemed she was encouraging his advances. After all, she hadn't exactly run away when she'd had the chance. It must have seemed obvious to him— even blatant—and yet, at the time, she had felt like a fly caught in a web, unable to move, let alone escape.

Yet again she stiffened her resolution to avoid him at all costs. Yet again, she felt only marginally better. Evade Dai Rees, she just might; evade the issues he had brought to the surface, she suspected she never would.

The case came up on the hottest day so far. Gina arrived at the Court hoping she looked cooler and more efficient than she felt. Reassuring an agitated Peggy did nothing to improve her own composure, as they sat in the drab waiting-room surrounded by other, equally jumpy defendants and their lawyers.

'When will it be our turn?' Peggy moaned, for the fourth time.

Gina glanced at her watch. 'Won't be long now, I'm sure.'

Jim sat close to his wife, one hand comfortingly on her knee. 'You're doing fine, old duck. Just a bit longer, and it'll all be over. They'll be getting through them other cases as fast as they can—won't they, Mrs Barton?'

'Of course they will. They always do this—tell everyone to come at the same time, then keep them waiting. Cruel, isn't it?'

'Like in hospitals,' suggested Jim, in a manful but misplaced attempt to take his wife's mind off her present dilemma. 'One clinic I went to, I was there all . . .'

'Oh Jim!' Peggy was close to tears. 'I won't be able to say a single word!'

'Don't worry so, Mrs Haines.' Gina wished she could soothe her own nerves as confidently as her client's. 'Just answer all the questions as accurately as you can. Tell them exactly what happened—as you remember it.'

'That's just the trouble,' wailed Peggy. 'I hardly do remember it. It's like a bad dream, all those weeks ago . . .'

'Well, remember everything we've said about it since. Just listen carefully to the question and give a truthful answer. That's all you can be expected to do. No one in their right mind could believe you capable of intending to steal, when they hear the whole story— wait and see.'

At last they were called; and after that, in Gina's later memories, the next hour always merged into a peculiar blur. Usually so clear-headed, she seemed today to lose her grip on reality, going through the motions—familiar, long-rehearsed questions and arguments—like an automaton. She knew she was doing her best; but it was all hazy, fuzzy at the edges—a badly-tuned television picture.

There was Peggy in the witness box, twisting her fingers together in an agony of nerves; and the store detective, poker-faced, inhuman; the young police officer who had carried out the arrest, reeling off the same formula of accusations he made, no doubt, ten times a week; and Jim, a pale face peering anxiously from the public seats, straining to catch his wife's every muttered syllable.

And there were the three Magistrates—two elderly men and a younger woman—sitting solemnly at their high Bench; earnest, intimidating, listening carefully and scribbling the odd note. At least, two of them were listening carefully; the third—one of the elderly men—appeared, to some irreverent and irrelevant corner of Gina's mind, to be fast asleep, like the Dormouse in Alice in Wonderland. Doubtless he was taking it all in as acutely as his colleagues, she told herself sardonically.

The charges were read, the cross-examinations completed, the details summed up; and the Magistrates retired to consider their verdict. For five minutes or so an uneasy silence prevailed, broken by whisperings and rustlings. 'Was it all right?' Peggy murmured faintly beside her; and Gina smiled as warmly as possible to assure her that it was.

Then they were all exhorted to Be Upstanding in Court for the return of the Magistrates, and Gina could feel the tension mounting as they took their seats again. The woman spoke for the Bench. The exact phrases she used in voicing their conclusions were lost on Gina—the rigid, conventional format she had heard dozens of times before. Only one word, the one meaningful sound among it all, stood out like the proverbial sore thumb from the rest: *Guilty*. They had lost.

For a few moments she was utterly shattered. Her self-esteem lay in ruins about her feet—shredded, deflated. She had done her best; but her best hadn't been good enough against this unbending system. She had let herself down; worse than that, she had let Peggy Haines down. The Courtroom reeled and spun around her head as the full implications of the verdict came home to her: for the sake of her own obstinate need to prove a point—to whom? to herself? to Dai Rees?—she had sacrificed Peggy's chances of being acquitted.

The benefit of presumption of innocence until guilt be proved ... the great, basic tenet of British law—the oldest, most respected legal structure in the history of the modern world. And now guilt had been proved—or had it? Was Peggy guilty of theft, just because this Court had found her so? Gina felt her resources gathering again: this wasn't the end, not by any means. There was a long way to go yet.

Outside the chamber, she turned to face her clients for the first time. White-faced and shaking, Peggy leaned on her husband's arm. Gina looked at them both, and her heart was filled with pity and remorse—but her determination set hard, stronger than ever. 'Mrs Haines—Mr Haines—I'm so very sorry,' she said quietly. From her tone and expression it was obvious how sincerely she meant it.

Jim shrugged. 'It wasn't your fault, Mrs Barton. I don't suppose we stood much of a chance. You did what you could, and we're grateful.'

Peggy was in a kind of dazed shock, but she nodded bravely. 'We're grateful,' she echoed. Then she swayed, and Jim's arm supported her round the waist, guiding her to one of the long seats round the edge of the waiting-room.

'Here, come on ducks, we can't have this. Come and sit down over here—that's the way—not to worry, it's not the end of the world ... only a small fine ...'

Gina followed and sat beside them. They were so sweet: even in their stunned state they didn't blame her. As far as they were concerned, it couldn't have been helped. But she had her own conscience to live with; the knowledge that she had refused to call in Counsel, for her own personal reasons—quite unconnected with the actual case. She wasn't going to dwell on that for the rest of her life—not if she could help it.

'Listen, Mrs Haines,' she began—as gently as she could, but unable to keep the urgent note from her voice. 'We don't have to leave it here. If you agree, we can take it further.'

Peggy had broken down now, and was weeping copiously into Jim's handkerchief. Jim's arm tightened around her, but his eyes were sharp on Gina's face. 'Further? You mean this isn't final, sort of thing?'

She nodded. 'Exactly. It doesn't have to be. It can be a long haul, but if you're prepared to be patient, we can appeal.'

'Appeal?' He frowned.

'That's right. Take it to a higher Court . . . probably the Crown Court. To be heard before a judge and jury.'

'You mean, like we could have done in the first place?'

'That's it,' Gina confirmed. 'We thought—my partners and I—that your case stood a good chance—or no worse a chance—at this Court than a higher one. But we might have been wrong, and it's not too late. If we disagree with this verdict we have every right to appeal against it, all the way up to the House of Lords if necessary. I think we should, Mr Haines,' she declared persuasively.

'Well . . .' He glanced at his wife, who was still sobbing bitterly. 'I don't know . . . she takes on so . . . she takes it all very hard, Mrs Barton.' There was just the faintest suggestion of reproach in his tone; Gina knew she deserved it, but she winced.

'Of course she does; anyone would. This whole thing must be like a nightmare for her.' She laid an emphatic hand on his arm. 'I really did think we'd get her off, Mr Haines. I really did hope . . . but it's no good looking back. Why don't we go forward? We'll help you all we can; I won't leave you in the lurch, I promise.'

'Would we need a—a barrister next time?'

'Yes, you would.' Gina's gaze dropped to her hands.

'I'm not saying—you know—we should've had one this time,' he assured her politely. 'I'm sure no one could've done it any better than you.'

Gina wished she had his confidence; but she said

nothing. Peggy had calmed herself a little, and was dabbing at her red puffy eyes. Crumpling the handkerchief into a soggy white ball, she looked up at Gina, sniffing. 'Did you say I could ... take it further, Mrs Barton?' she croaked.

'That's right, Peg,' Jim interposed. 'We can appeal, Mrs Barton says. What do you think? Could you go through it all again?' There was doubt in his tone, but hope too.

'It might take months to come up,' Gina warned. 'But we'd get you the best Counsel, and a Jury is often more understanding than Magistrates, in cases like this.'

Peggy Haines gazed at her husband, and then at her solicitor. Both were staring at her, their expressions intense, questioning. She made up her mind. 'Yes, I want to appeal against it.' She nodded vehemently. 'Definitely. I'm not guilty and I won't let them say I am. Not without a fight.'

Moved almost to tears herself, Gina reached over to squeeze her client's hand. 'Well done, Peggy. It's the right decision, I'm sure of it.'

Jim gave his wife a hug. 'That's my brave girl. You're a fighter, Peg—always were. Always had spirit, my Peg,' he informed Gina proudly. 'We'll show 'em, eh, Mrs Barton?'

Gina smiled at them both, her mind suddenly clear and razor-sharp. 'We'll show them, Mr Haines. And whatever happens, at least we'll always know we did everything we could.'

When Gina reported back to the office at lunchtime, Sam and Brian took one look at her pale, tense face and dragged her off round the corner to the local pub. Neither of them said a word until she was safely established at a table and Sam had gone off to buy the drinks.

'No need to ask how it went.' Brian was scrutinising her anxiously. 'Bad, was it?'

'Not really. I mean, there was nothing traumatic about the hearing itself—it went off okay, just like any other hearing. Quite routine. No . . .' she faltered; it was impossible to explain to the well-meaning Brian just why she was so affected.

Sam arrived, bearing three full glasses on a tray. 'Get this down you, love—put some roses back in your cheeks—I hate to see my Gina looking so low.'

She smiled wanly as she sipped her dry sherry. 'Do I look as bad as that? I've lost cases before—and doubtless will again—I've got no business to feel so cut up over this one.'

'This one means a lot to you, and you know it.' Sam sat down and took a swig of draught bitter. Brian glanced from one to the other, puzzled; but he said nothing. 'Don't forget, Gina,' Sam continued, 'shop-lifting cases are notoriously tough nuts to crack. By far the majority don't get off. You were brave to have a go, but . . .' he spread his hands philosophically.

'I never had a hope?' Gina's spirit was returning, along with her colour. There was challenge in the gaze she directed at Sam.

'I didn't say that. But it would have been a notable achievement if you'd won.'

'What are you going to do—leave it there?' Brian enquired, his nose emerging from his tankard.

'No way. We're appealing against it,' she announced mutinously.

'Good for you!' Sam exclaimed at once. 'And the clients agree to this?'

'They're all for it. I persuaded them to stick up for their rights, and Peggy Haines is no wet blanket. She was upset, of course, but she soon snapped out of it when she realised we hadn't reached the end.'

'You'll need to brief Counsel this time,' remarked Brian blandly. 'Going to give the great Rees another try?'

'See if he'll recant his chauvinist views?' added Sam with a twinkle.

They both stared at her expectantly; she took her time, finishing her sherry and setting the empty schooner deliberately down on the table. 'Not a chance,' she told them. 'The Old Bailey will collapse sooner than that man's prejudices. No—I'll have to book John Slade when he gets back—make sure he's able to take it on. Nothing but the best for my clients,' she declared, leaning back and folding her arms in a gesture of defiance.

Brian's air of faint bewilderment deepened; he had never seen this aspect of Gina in action. Sam grinned and collected their glasses together. 'Who's for another? How about a cheese roll, Gina—further fortifications? Can't have you losing strength—you'll need all you've got for the battle ahead.'

She considered. 'I'll have a scotch egg, please Sam, and a bowl of Mavis's home-made soup if there's any left. But,' she insisted, 'it's my round. I'll see to the drinks while you buy snacks.'

'I never argue with a lady—especially when she's buying me a beer,' agreed Sam solemnly. 'Wonderful thing, equality,' he commented to Brian as Gina made her way towards the bar.

Halfway through the afternoon, when she was scratching her head over a particularly tricky divorce settlement, the 'phone rang on Gina's desk, and Michele's voice enquired whether she was free to speak to Mr Dai Rees.

Dai Rees? What on earth could he want? 'He certainly chooses his moments,' she grumbled into the mouthpiece. 'All right, Michele—better put him through.'

The familiar deep tones resonated in the receiver. She gripped it tightly, willing her foolish body not to respond to them—a vain hope, it turned out. 'Gina? Is that you?'

'Yes, Mr Rees?'

He sighed audibly. 'I thought we'd got past all that

Mr and *Mrs* business. What have I done wrong this time?'

'Wrong?' she echoed coldly. 'How do you mean?'

'You know very well what I mean. I wasn't exactly number one in the popularity ratings, but I thought I'd cleaned my copybook up a bit since then.'

'Did you?' She did her best to sound flippant rather than brittle.

'I did. But it appears I was mistaken.'

'Mr Rees—Dai—I'm very busy today. Is there something I can do for you?'

'Now there's an interesting offer. Can I have it in writing, Mrs Barton?'

She blushed, thanking God she was alone in her office. 'If this is a social call, I suggest . . .'

'No, Gina,' he interrupted. 'It's not a social call— not entirely, at least. I've just heard about your hearing this morning.'

So the grape vine had already been buzzing, had it? Bad news travels fastest, her mind taunted cynically. 'Oh yes?' she said cautiously. 'Got your ear to the ground over there, haven't you?'

'I like to keep abreast of events,' he agreed crisply. 'The Clerk to that Court is a friend of mine, as it happens. Anyway, I knew the case came up today—I was keeping an eye on the lists . . .'

'Ready to pounce on an opportunity to crow?' she challenged sarcastically. 'Well, aren't you going to say you told me so? *"I won't say I warned you, but I did, didn't I?"*' she mimicked, with unusual bitterness. This was all she needed—to have her nose rubbed in her failure by the great man himself—the great man who would have done so much better, had she allowed him to plead the case on her behalf.

But his reply was unexpected—the tone sympathetic. 'I can imagine how you must be feeling, Gina. You'd . . . set a certain store by it, I know. But you mustn't feel personally responsible . . . that's a recipe for disaster in this business. You must look ahead, to the next case—it's the only way.'

Gina was far from mollified by his kindly advice; she would, for some obscure reason, have preferred his normal brusqueness. 'Thanks for the words of wisdom, Mr Rees—I'll bear them in mind. Good of you to spare the time to patronise a poor, unsuccessful, insignificant solicitor—and a female one at that.'

'No need to resort to acerbity, my dear,' he returned levelly—only fuelling her irritation. 'I assure you my intentions were honourable: I was simply hoping to offer encouragement and support to a colleague at what I imagined might be her hour of need. I can see now,' he concluded drily, 'that they were misplaced.'

All at once Gina felt worn out and ashamed. What was the point of all this friction between them—what good did it do anyone? She had neither seen nor heard from him since those moments out of time in Jackie's garden, three weeks ago. If she was brutally honest, she had to acknowledge a thread of disappointment interlaced with her relief when he hadn't contacted her. 'I apologise, Dai,' she said wearily. 'I'm—I don't know—rather tired. It was rather a strain,' she confessed. 'And of course I'm disappointed to have lost.'

'Naturally you are. I accept your apology, Gina. You feel things deeply, don't you?' There was a pause, during which she failed to think up a suitably impersonal reply to this highly personal remark. 'Anyway,' he went on briskly, 'I 'phoned to ask what you intend to do about it now? You'll appeal, won't you?'

'Yes. We've already decided to.'

'Good. You'll need Counsel then, to take it to Crown Court?'

She knew what was coming next. 'Yes, Dai, but . . .'

He brushed any objections aside. 'Well, consider me hired.'

Gina drew several deep breaths before she replied— carefully, calmly. 'No, Dai. I can't take back my decision—not unless you can change your attitude.'

'Gina!' Exasperation all but overthrew his studied courtesy. 'I'm ... how many years older than you? Seven? Eight? I've been around a long time; I've formed extremely firm and positive views about the world. No one—but *no one*,' he emphasised, 'is going to walk into my life and change them, just like that. Maybe I made a mistake when I divulged them to you . . .'

'Maybe you did,' she conceded flatly.

'. . . but it's done now, and I don't go back on what I've said; and I can't pretend to, either. Not for anyone; ever.'

'Well,' she observed, after a slight pause, 'that seems to just about sum it up then, doesn't it?'

'Impasse?' he suggested.

'Yes.'

'The immovable object and the irresistible force?'

'Something like that, yes.'

'Okay, Gina.' Suddenly he was lightly humorous again. 'I don't believe in pushing in where I'm not wanted. But does the immovable object extend her impenetrability to other areas of her life?'

'What sort of areas?' she hedged suspiciously.

'Would I be a little less resistible if I asked you out to dinner?'

She swallowed hard. 'Well, I don't know, Dai ... I . . .'

'Babysitting problems? A busy social schedule? Work to do in the evenings—with colleague Gillow, perhaps?' The satirical excuses hurled themselves down the telephone at her.

She sat up straight, holding the receiver away from her ear and scowling at it as if it had bitten her. Then she opened her handbag and took out her diary. 'I'd be pleased to accept your invitation,' she told him coolly. 'When did you have in mind?'

CHAPTER SIX

SHE had been right about Dai's car. *Fast, smooth and expensive*, she had guessed; and the dark red Lancia now waiting on the yellow line opposite her house shouted that it was all three. Ruggedly sophisticated like the man who owned it; smart and yet functional, without unnecessary ostentation. Gina was impressed—but not even by the merest flicker of an eyelash did she let Dai know that.

Instead she stopped at the top of the short flight of steps leading from her door. 'How about letting me drive you in my Metro?' she suggested sweetly.

He was already halfway down the steps ahead of her, car-keys in his right hand. Now he swung round to face her—mouth set hard, eyes tempered steel as they studied her with renewed intensity. They seemed to engulf her, following the line of her simple summer dress—surely penetrating right through to the unprotected curves beneath . . . but she stood her ground, maintaining her serene expression as his gaze came to rest upon it.

'And why the hell should I do that?' he demanded.

She raised her eyebrows just a fraction. 'Oh, I don't know—I just thought—perhaps you might like to hand over the wheel for once. Or you might like to drink more than me—I don't indulge heavily,' she explained blandly. 'Then you wouldn't have to worry about driving home afterwards.'

He thrust both hands deep into the pockets of his close-fitting slacks, still jingling the keys. The cutting edge to his tone was positively serrated. 'I'm not in the habit of over-indulging,' he assured her tersely. 'Nor of allowing women to chauffeur me about. So, if you will permit me . . .' Turning again, he strode across the road to open the passenger door of his car and wait, with exaggerated chivalry, while she followed him and climbed in. Then he marched round to his own side and got in next to her.

Gina fastened her seat-belt and leaned back, appreciating the streamlined comfort of the Lancia's interior, the responsive way it sprang into life at Dai's touch and purred away from the kerb. Neither of them spoke again until they were well on their way through the busy early-evening streets. He drove confidently, decisively, as she supposed he must do most things. 'I'm sorry,' she ventured, 'if my offer offended you. It wasn't meant to.'

Dai's glance conveyed scepticism, but he managed a half-smile. 'No offence taken, Mrs Burton. It just happens to be something I feel strongly about, that's all.'

'Being driven around by women?'

'Being driven around by anyone, really. I like to be in charge. Arrogant of me, no doubt, but I prefer to be in control of my own destiny.'

'Particularly,' she persisted—keeping her tone light and restrained—'if control looks like passing into female hands?'

'Perhaps I don't feel entirely safe in the fair hands of a lady driver,' he admitted cautiously, his eyes fixed on the road. 'To quote your mother's native language at you, I've always worked on the assumption that *La Donna è Mobile*.'

'It's just as well I understand Italian,' Gina observed, 'or I might think you meant "the lady is mobile", rather than "unpredictable"—which would rather undermine your point.'

He grinned. 'It's the ones who are mobile *and* unpredictable who are the menaces. Female motorists, in other words.'

Bristling inwardly, Gina held on to her veneer of rational calm. 'Well, that view certainly tallies with the interesting prejudices you expressed at our first meeting.'

Braking the car smoothly at a red light, he turned to look her full in the face. 'Gina,' he appealed—his voice low and persuasive, 'let's call a truce for tonight, shall we? I didn't ask you out so that we could wrangle. Let's agree to disagree—and keep off all matters legal, just for a few hours?' When she said nothing, he continued on a more strident note, 'I've already told you—I'm not about to change the attitudes of a lifetime. And I ought to warn you, before we go any further—I'm totally immune to proselytising. All previous attempts at conversion have failed dismally. If you can't accept me the way I am . . .' he shrugged, letting the handbrake off as the traffic crept forwards.

'. . . I don't have to accept you at all?' she completed, sardonically.

He inclined his head slightly. 'My case rests, Your Honour.'

Her sidelong glance took in the firmly chiselled profile—impassive under the undisciplined black mane which curled over his shirt collar at the back. Switching her gaze quickly in the opposite direction, she settled further into the deep leather seat, watching through the tinted window as London night-life swung into action. 'Okay, Dai.' She forced her mind not to dwell on all those 'previous attempts at conversion'. 'I'll be only too glad not to talk shop this evening—goodness knows I could do with a break from it all. And I'll do my best not to . . . proselytise; but I can't promise. I've got some fairly strong opinions too,' she reminded him.

'I'm fully aware of that.' Dry amusement brought a twitch to his mouth, a glint to his eye. 'I may be a lost cause, but that doesn't prevent me from picking up a gauntlet when one is thrown directly at me.'

'Is that what I am?' She looked at him thoughtfully. 'A challenge?'

'Of course—to some extent. Life would be an empty affair without them, don't you think?'

'I suppose so.' For a few moments she was silent,

considering the implications of the role, and wondering whether she liked them.

'If you're honest, Gina,' he pressed, 'you'll admit you're here for the same reason.'

'Because you're a challenge?'

'Precisely.' Again she remained silent. 'You see,' he went on quietly, 'you can't deny it.'

She stared through the window again, and decided to change the subject. 'Where are we going? I presume our destination has been firmly fixed—without benefit of democratic discussion?'

'Didn't you want it to be?' he countered instantly.

This was certainly a poser. Gina was quite unused to having such minor decisions—or indeed any decisions—taken out of her hands. When she and Brian went out together, he was content to leave the arrangements to her—and as often as not, the transport as well. Even when they seemed to come to a conclusion jointly, she usually had the feeling afterwards that his part in it had been, in some obscure way, subordinate to her own. It had been the same with Pete, all those years ago: he had been perfectly happy to leave everyday responsibilities to Gina.

Since then, she had always preferred the company of men who did just that. Unassuming men, who treated her with a kind of deference; encouraged her to take up the reins, respecting her wishes and judgments above their own. She had always thought she liked it— liked men—that way. So why didn't she just say so, now, in uncompromising terms? Could it be that an element of excitement—almost of relief—had got itself mixed in with her disapproval of Dai Rees's strongarm tactics? She was appalled at the idea.

'Well?' he was insisting, as she failed to find a reply. '*Is* that how you want it? Democracy in all things? Equality at any price?'

'It might make a change,' she said at last, 'to see how the other half lives.'

'To see what those poor downtrodden sisters of

yours have to put up with, you mean?' Wicked humour underlined the question. 'Well, just this once, Gina, I'm taking you out to dinner; and there's going to be no argument about who's paying, or where we're going, or who's driving. All right?'

'And am I allowed to choose what I want to eat,' she enquired mildly, 'when we get there?'

'Oh, I think we might let you do that—if you're a very good girl and don't argue any more.'

'Well then, where *are* we going?'

'What do you like eating?' Once again her query was parried with another.

She deliberated. 'I like virtually anything, as long as it's well-cooked: Italian, French, English, Chinese, Indian, Greek, Indonesian, Japanese . . .' she reeled off the possibilities nonchalantly, indicating that her cosmopolitan lifestyle had encompassed them all on a regular basis—an unjustifiable claim.

'Say no more,' he interrupted. 'I had the feeling your main interest would be in the quality of the food itself, so I've booked us in at a small Bistro I've got to know—not far from my flat, actually—perhaps you know it?'

'Perhaps I do,' she agreed doubtfully, thinking of the many good restaurants in an area noted for them.

'Just an informal place,' he explained. 'I've visited it several times since I came to London. The cooking's outstanding—I'm sure you'll like it. Does that sound suitable to Madame?' he mocked.

'It sounds highly suitable,' she assured him primly.

It was, in the event, highly suitable. In fact it was just the kind of place Gina liked best: cosy and candlelit, welcoming and yet discreet; where taste and service were all-important but no one pressed their unwanted attentions on you. Where the *patron* greeted Dai like an old friend, and made a few quiet suggestions and recommendations about his menu, but after that remained tactfully in the background—no more than a genial, hospitable presence. Where the music was played live by a bearded young man on an acoustic guitar: an assortment of folk and classical melodies which echoed delicately, soulfully across the small space, winding their subtle way between tables—never obtrusive but infinitely effective.

Gina opted for two of her favourite dishes: mushrooms *à la Grècque* and Boeuf Bourguignonne. Dai chose French onion soup and a steak au poivre. Without consulting her, he also ordered a bottle of young Beaujolais. 'Should go well with this lot, I think.' He snapped the wine list shut with an air of finality. As it happened, Gina was no expert on that subject, so she held her peace.

While they ate their *hors d'oeuvres*, they eyed each other warily—conscious of a mutual attempt to keep conversation at a detached, chatty level. Gradually, as they loosened up, so did communications between them—ranging over a wide variety of impersonal topics: politics, the arts, their respective outside interests. Again, Gina marvelled at how easy, how relaxed it all was—how often they found themselves in agreement—once they steered clear of those deeper, more dangerous waters.

Tonight, Dai was deliberately displaying a different side of his nature: sensitive charm to the fore, abrasive aggression left far behind. Even as Gina revelled in the new feelings of warmth he evoked, she could sense those earlier warnings receding into the distance—out of earshot, out of mind . . .

She glanced at the man sitting opposite her, now tucking into his steak and vegetables; and it was as if she had known him for years. The Beaujolais—which was proving to be exceedingly easy to drink—liberated and lubricated certain areas of her mind, even as it closed off certain others. She realised with a shock that—on the contrary—she hardly knew him at all. He knew a great deal about her; and she knew next to nothing about him. That was a situation which would have to be rectified, she decided, before the night was much older.

She laid down her fork. 'Delicious beef,' she remarked with a smile.

'Good.' He returned the smile, raising his glass to her. 'So is mine. Like the wine?'

'Lovely. It's all lovely, Dai. Thanks.'

'Glad it meets with the Barton seal of approval.' He left her in no doubt that he had known it would. Even in this gentler mood, he oozed confidence from every pore.

'Tell me about yourself,' she demanded suddenly, leaning forward to gaze earnestly into his face.

He was almost taken off guard; but not quite. 'What a woman!' He threw up his hands in satirical horror. 'She gets me here, all softened up with food and drink and candlelight and music—and then begins the inquisition.'

'No inquisition,' she denied emphatically. 'Just that I've told you a lot about me, and you've kept suspiciously quiet about the real David Rees.'

'David, is it now?' The heavy black brows shot up. 'Well, there's formal,' he added, in exaggeratedly Welsh accents. 'What do you want to know about, little Mrs B.? My murky and sordid past? My depraved adulthood, or my deprived childhood?'

'We could start with the latter,' she suggested— though the former sounded a good deal more fascinating.

He leaned back in his chair. 'I was born at a very early age,' he informed her—the grey eyes taking on a far-away expression as he made a great show of casting his memory back to long-forgotten times.

She nodded gravely. 'Yet another thing we have in common,' she pointed out. 'And after that?'

'I grew up, still at an early age. My father,' he went on, becoming marginally more serious, 'was a miner. I was brought up in the Valleys, not far from Pontypool. Have you ever,' he enquired, 'been to Pontypool?'

'I'm afraid not.' She sipped her wine, warm brown eyes fixed encouragingly on his face.

'No, I don't suppose you would have. Well, my old man was a miner all his life.'

'Was?'

He nodded briefly. 'He died ten years ago—pneumoconiosis.' Anger flickered across his features. 'The coal dust got him.'

'And your mother?' Intrigued now, Gina willed him to go on.

'Still very much alive—and kicking. Still in the village, minding everyone else's business. Keeps tabs on all of them, does my mam.' There was a softening of affection in his expression now, and pride.

'Any others in the family?'

'Oh yes—two brothers and a sister. Brothers both down the mine; sister married to a miner. I was the one that got away,' he explained bluntly.

'How did you manage it?' She was genuinely riveted by these unexpected revelations. Some of his character, at least, was falling into place.

'Sheer determination—and slog. Got to the top at school, decided which profession to go for—and went for it.'

He made it sound so simple. 'But law—that's the most difficult profession of all to rise in without some ... backing.' Gina couldn't disguise her admiration. 'How did you do it?' she repeated.

Suddenly he was concentrating hard on refilling their glasses with the last of the wine. 'As I said, Gina—hard work. And plain, unadulterated brilliance, of course,' he added, with the old gleam of arrogance. 'It wasn't easy,' he admitted, as she continued to gaze at him searchingly, 'but once I set my sights on a thing ...' (*or a person*, the unvoiced phrase hung in the air between them) '... I usually achieve my ambition in the end. How about another of these?' he suggested smoothly.

Gina glanced down at the empty bottle. 'Not for me,

thanks. I've had more than enough.' Her mind was still racing over his story. 'But you must have had to finance yourself somehow, through to your pupillage. Once you were through college—that's when it gets expensive, isn't it? Before actually being called to the Bar?'

He frowned, as if reluctant to pursue the subject. 'It was a challenging time, yes. But I hope I've already made it clear that I enjoy a challenge. I took any night job I could get, that first year of vocational training— I've been a waiter, a petrol pump attendant, a messenger. Anything which left me free in the daytime to study and sit the exams. No . . .' his mouth quirked in a rueful half-grin, 'it wasn't easy.'

'And after the first year?' She was avid, now, to find out more. 'Did you have to go on moonlighting until you'd got started in practice?'

He turned to summon the waiter. Gina had the distinct impression he was evading her question. 'Shall we have a sweet?' he invited as the waiter hovered. 'They do a wonderful desserts trolley here.'

She dragged her mind back to the immediate present. 'Yes please. I can't resist those strawberries— I noticed them as we came in.'

'And I'll have profiteroles,' Dai told the waiter. 'And two coffees. And a brandy?' he asked Gina. 'Or a liqueur?'

'I wouldn't mind a Grand Marnier,' she accepted, surprising herself. 'To round off a superb meal.' She smiled at the waiter.

He beamed, enchanted by the compliment. 'I shall inform Chef,' he announced happily, 'that the food met with your satisfaction.' Then he trotted off to find the desserts trolley.

Dai appeared to be lost in his own contemplations. 'You were about to tell me . . .' Gina reminded him.

'Was I?' His brow furrowed. 'Tell you what?'

'Don't prevaricate, Dai. I was really interested. How you managed for the rest of your training—

without family or means to support you. Did you have to work your way right through it?'

He stared at her; it was almost as if he was staring right through her. 'No,' he said at last. 'I didn't have to. I had . . . help.'

The more unwilling he was to divulge further details, the more intrigued she became. 'What sort of help? A sponsor?'

'I suppose you could put it that way,' he agreed drily. The waiter arrived with their coffee, desserts and liqueurs—saving Dai once again from expanding on a theme which he was clearly reluctant to follow up.

Biding her time, Gina ate a strawberry. 'Mmm— delicious. Well?' she persisted.

'Well?' he echoed, cutting into a profiterole swimming in rich chocolate.

Gina's dark gaze was penetrating. 'Is it something you don't want to tell me?'

'Full marks, Mrs Barton. You must be an ace when it comes to cross-examination,' he commented lightly, 'with this grim resolve to get to the bottom of everything—and everyone.'

She subsided, strangely deflated. His defence had taken the form of an attack, which had reached a currently vulnerable spot. 'Not exactly an ace,' she muttered, 'as you well know.' Then she rallied, renewing her own attack. She was blowed if she'd let herself be steam-rollered by him now—not having got this far. She changed her approach to one of playful teasing. 'I can't believe your cupboard conceals a skeleton so shameful you can't tell me about it.'

'It's not that it's shameful. It's just not a subject I like to bandy about.' Without warning, he reached across the table top to take her hand in his own— broad fingers enclosing small ones completely. 'Do we have to talk about this here and now, Gina? I'm enjoying your company more than I can say . . . don't spoil the evening.'

He was leaning towards her—intimate, intense—pulling her into that magnetic field he seemed to carry about with him. A range of emotions flooded her—among them just a touch of remorse. 'I'm sorry, Dai. I didn't mean to dig—not if it hurts. Of course you don't have to tell me until—unless—you want to . . .' Her curiosity had been sharply aroused; but—if he felt as strongly as all that—it would have to wait.

The fingers were stroking hers—lightly brushing her skin with their square tips. If he had kicked her hard, the physical impact couldn't have been more total. 'I know I don't, Gina. And just at this moment, I'm not going to. I might one day—but not now; now is for you and me. Okay?'

'Okay.' Her breath had become shallow; she felt herself mesmerised by those acute eyes that were now levelled so intently on to her own.

He released her hand abruptly in order to pick up his balloon glass and inhale the bouquet of the Cognac before drinking it. The momentary tension dispelled, they steered the conversation carefully back to neutral territory— sharing the last of their meal in the same companionable mood in which they had started it.

'Coming back to see my flat?' he invited coolly, as they reached the car.

She didn't bother to hide her grin. 'And your collection of etchings?'

'Not a single etching,' he assured her solemnly. 'But some quite good coffee.'

'I couldn't eat—or drink—another thing. What I really could do with now,' she said firmly, 'is a short walk.'

'Excellent idea. How about a stroll up Primrose Hill itself? Lovely at night—but you'll know all about that, veteran Londoner as you are.'

'A bit less of the veteran, if you don't mind. But I've been up there a few times, yes. That sounds just right.'

Leaving the car where it was, they made their way through now-darkened streets, past rows of decidedly up-market shops, to where the grassy mound loomed over the urban landscape. Its foothills were gentle green slopes, leading to a children's playground—and then to the edge of the Zoo, where Lord Snowdon's angular, space-age aviary could just be made out, an eerie shape in the darkness.

They set off along a path lined with original Victorian gas-lamps—no longer burning gas, but preserving a quaintly authentic sense of history about the place. Down here, they weren't alone: a motley assortment of nocturnal ramblers shared the path— self-absorbed couples, late-night dog-walkers, fanatic joggers. As they reached the steeper gradient near the summit, they left most of their fellow ramblers behind; and the soft night air was already taking over—enfolding them into a tiny private world.

Reaching a point near the top, they left the relative brightness of the path to walk across the dewy grass and stand in silence among the shadows. There was nothing Victorian about the great city which sprawled away below them—so near and yet so separate; neon-flared skyscrapers scarring and obscuring a skyline which still included—if you looked carefully—the ancient course of the Thames, the old familiar outlines of St Paul's and Big Ben. The sight was always magical, especially on warm nights; and Gina felt herself caught up in the spell that was London—proud to be part of its throbbing complexity, but relieved to be surveying it, at this moment, from a safe distance.

She turned shining eyes to Dai, and at exactly the same second he tore his own gaze from that view to look down at her. The smiles they exchanged in the faint starlight were strangely secret, conspiratorial—as if they were borrowing time from their own better natures...acting against their own better judgements.

Then Dai's arm was around her shoulders, pulling her to him, turning her slowly to face him; and when she didn't resist, his other hand was lifting her chin, so that she was forced to stare straight up into that powerful, shaded face.

'Mrs Barton,' he murmured, his grey gaze never leaving her soft mouth as he moved inexorably towards it, 'your company—this place—the combination is potent. I shan't forget it.'

Gina was only too well aware that she would never forget it, either. But she had no time to say so before his lips were claiming hers—at first tentatively, experimentally, recalling that earlier, subtle statement of intent.

Then, as if a tightly clamped lid had been lifted and a storm of passion broken loose, he was muttering her name against her mouth, prising it open with his tongue to taste and explore and plunder its sweetness until the stars left the sky to invade her closed eyes and dance inside her head.

One of his hands was at the small of her back, grinding her—soft, pliant—against his rising tautness—heaping fuel on the flames which already surged uncontrollably within her body. The other clasped her neck, fingers tangling painfully in her hair so that the neat, glossy coil loosened itself to cascade down her back in straight strands of deep chestnut. She never knew how they had made the descent to the sloping ground; only that they were there on the lush damp grass, still welded together—lips, arms, bodies still clinging as if separation would mean death.

His mouth had become part of hers—dragging from it responses she had forgotten herself capable of—rekindling fires which she had thought long-extinguished. Her arms wound themselves round his neck, urging him closer, making demands of their own. Leaving her back, his hand crept up to explore her face, neck, shoulder; then one firm rounded breast—palm and fingers teasing it to wanton life through the insubstantial cotton of her dress.

She tore her lips from his, gasping; but he

recaptured them to begin all over again, as if he was
feeding a furious craving in them both. She was
drowned, drugged—lost in the sensations he aroused.
Her mind recognised no part of them as hers; her
heart and body knew better.

At last her mind's anxious messages percolated
through the red haze. After all, it lectured demurely,
they weren't even alone; they were in a public place,
even if it was a dark and semi-deserted one. With a
superhuman effort, she eluded Dai's devouring mouth
again, pushing with all her strength against the
unyielding wall of his chest. 'Dai—please!' Her voice
was shaky; and so—when she scrambled to her feet,
smoothing her clothes, making a futile attempt to tidy
her hair—were her legs.

Instantly he was upright beside her, steadying her
with a hand on each shoulder. 'Gina! What's the
matter? It's all right . . . don't run away from me . . .'

She stared at the ground, unable to meet his
piercing gaze. 'It's just—there are people around—I
feel . . . exposed.'

He laughed, deep in his throat. 'You weren't half as
exposed to them as you were to me, Gina.' She
flushed, grateful for the enveloping darkness. 'All
passers-by can see is yet another courting couple,
harmlessly enjoying a cuddle in the grass. In this
light—and in this day and age—they're hardly likely to
stop and make a detailed investigation of the
proceedings. Not unless they're salacious small boys,'
he added, 'and I doubt whether many of those are
about at this hour.'

She could scarcely argue with the logic of this. 'All
the same,' she murmured, 'I think I'd like to go home
now.'

He pulled her close to peer at her face in the gloom.
'You're not really upset, are you, Gina?' When she
tried to turn her head away, he captured her chin with
one strong hand, forcing her to look at him. 'It wasn't
exactly rape, you know. It takes two—and a certain

chemistry—to constitute a moment like that.' He
leaned even nearer and she saw light from her own
eyes, a faintly reflected gleam in the deep black circles
of his pupils. 'Did you really think you'd be safe
from—all that—if you summoned the protection of the
great outdoors?' He chuckled again—a low, almost
sinister sound. 'No way, Mrs B. You don't escape the
forces of nature that easily.'

His fingers bit into her soft cheeks; she could feel
her lips already swelling into bruises. She flinched—
but it was from his words, not his grasp. 'I know that,
Dai,' she whispered.

'You're not used to letting out your instincts like
that, are you?' he challenged softly. 'You've been
keeping them locked up, haven't you—firmly in their
place? What a crying shame,' he went on, almost to
himself. 'What a waste—all that warmth, and passion,
and humanity, kept under lock and key, waiting for
. . . waiting for what, Gina?'

She shook her head free of his hand, unable to
answer. 'Dai—please take me home,' she pleaded, on a
half-sob.

He gathered her into his arms then, as if she were a
child. Folded deep inside their strength, she knew a
sharp, overwhelming urge to let the world slip away,
with all its responsibilities and cares, leaving her to his
tender mercies. He would support her; fend off the
slings and arrows of outrageous fortune . . . he would
bring her to life, creating new vitality in her even as he
protected her. It could all be so simple: he was a man,
she was a woman, together they could form the perfect
partnership . . .

Horrified at such treacherous notions, her mind
took over and goaded her body into action. She broke
away from his embrace and took a step back, breathing
deeply. 'Take me home,' she repeated on a firmer
note.

'Don't worry, little lady. I'm not keeping you out all
night. We're both well past the age when the

greensward makes a suitable bower.' He made no attempt to touch her now, but stood regarding her from a short distance away with a clear glint of irony. 'Come on then—let's go.' And he swung round to set off back to the path at a brisk pace, leaving her to catch up.

As they walked down the hill side by side, he took her hand; and she made no pretence of withdrawing it. In spite of her mind's dismay at her body's weakness, there seemed little harm in such peripheral contact. She wished, she only wished, his hand didn't feel so right, so . . . fitting, wrapped possessively round hers.

In the car neither of them spoke until he drew up outside her house. It was well after midnight: all the windows were black and lifeless.

'No one home?' he asked in surprise. 'What about Toby? No babysitter?'

'Toby's away,' she informed him succinctly. 'I'm on my own for a few days.'

'Is that so?' He looked at her speculatively. 'Going to ask me in for that cup of coffee I never made you?'

For a brief, crazy second she was tempted; then she knew just how crazy it would have been. 'Not this time, Dai. I'm exhausted, and I have to go to work tomorrow.' The excuse sounded tame; that wasn't what her refusal was about, and they both knew it.

His eyes narrowed; then he spread his hands in a gesture of acceptance. 'You and me both. Ah well . . . win some, lose some,' he remarked philosophically.

I bet you don't lose many, Gina's mind taunted in its infuriating way; but all she said was: 'Thanks for a lovely evening.'

Once again he turned to take her face between his hands, gently this time, studying it in the glow from the streetlamps. 'Such polite, well-bred sentiments, Mrs Barton. Have you really enjoyed yourself?'

'I really have.' She smiled at him; there was no harm, surely, in admitting that. 'The meal was excellent. I must remember that place . . .'

'And afterwards?' he cut in, damming her nervous flow of small talk. 'Did you . . . enjoy that too?'

She swallowed. 'I can't . . . there's nothing I can say about that, Dai. It happened, that's all. One of those things that happen . . . the atmosphere . . . just one of those . . .'

'Nothing to do with you and me?' His thumbs were caressing her cheeks now in a soft circling motion, sending shivers through her whole body. 'Purely a matter of atmosphere?' His eyes gleamed wickedly in the half-light. 'Don't kid yourself, Gina. You know better than that. You haven't just fallen off the tree.' He leaned closer; she could feel his breath on her face. 'We're a symphony orchestra, you and me; we're . . . dynamite, a crashing, elemental explosion—only waiting to happen. I might be letting you go this time, but don't think I will indefinitely. You've got a whole lot of catching up to do—and I'm the man you're going to do it with.'

She drew in her breath sharply, twisting to escape from his grip. 'What makes you so sure of yourself?' she demanded—helplessness bringing its own defiance.

He released her. 'It's what makes the world go round. Nothing mysterious about it—it's the oldest, most basic human instinct of all. The only really potent force our godforsaken species has left to us. You're not going to miss out on your share of it, any more than I am.' On this matter-of-fact, almost bitter note, he started the engine. 'Run along then. Mustn't miss your beauty sleep. Or perhaps,' he conjectured cynically, 'you're more concerned with restoring your little grey cells than your external wrapping?'

She stared at him wide-eyed, momentarily stunned by this offhand dismissal. Then, gathering up her handbag and jacket along with her dignity, she opened the passenger door. 'Good night, Dai. I expect I'll see you again—sometime.'

'Of that, Gina,' he drawled as she climbed out, 'you

can be absolutely certain. Good night—sleep well.' He leaned over to slam the door shut behind her.

The Lancia's tail-lights receded to twin points in the distance. Gina stood in the midst of a resounding silence, on the deserted pavement outside her empty home.

CHAPTER SEVEN

By the end of the week the weather had broken. On the Friday—the day before she was due to set off for the Cotswolds—Gina sat at her desk, making a pretence of wading through a pile of correspondence but actually staring out at the leaden sky, the relentless rain making waterfalls down her window.

She sighed: strange how holidays provided a signal for the skies to open. It was so much more of a strain driving on wet roads—but she'd done it before often enough, and she supposed this time wouldn't be any worse. She'd been looking forward to a bit of sunbathing; but never mind—it would be a rest and a change, whatever the weather, and she could certainly do with both. A few days of her parents' undemanding, supportive company would help her to sort herself out—and God knew, she needed it. And it would be wonderful to see Toby again. The fortnight had gone quickly, but she really had missed him.

Smiling, she bent her head again to concentrate on her work. Immersed in the complex instructions of an elderly gentleman wishing to change his will for the fifth time at least, she jumped when the telephone shrilled out its strident demand close to her elbow. Leaning back in her chair, she picked up the receiver.

'Yes?'

'Gina?' The voice cut straight across the days, straight down the wires into secret corners of her body which twitched and churned as it reached them. She winced: she had just about managed to banish Dai Rees to the outer edges of her mind, where he belonged—during the day, at least—and now the good work was undone, all in a second.

'Dai! How did you get through to me? Michele is supposed to . . .'

'Guard you from unwelcome intrusions? I have my ways of dealing with such obstacles. I informed your charming secretary that it was a matter of some urgency, and I knew you wouldn't object if she connected me at once.'

'You did, did you?' That was him all over—charm the birds from the telegraph poles (and doubtless, her caustic mind added, charm a good deal more from them once he'd got them down). 'Well, I'd prefer it if you didn't.'

'I apologise for offending office protocol. I wanted to talk to you, and I haven't got time to waste drumming my fingers while you're prepared for the shock. Anyway,' he challenged, 'why should it matter? You haven't got any reason to try and avoid me, have you, Gina?'

'Of course not,' she replied, rather too quickly. 'But I'm busy, Dai, so if you'll tell me why you rang . . .'

'Always on the go, always on the run, our Mrs Barton,' he mocked irritatingly. 'Aren't you going to tell me how much you enjoyed our evening together?'

'I told you at the time,' she reminded him crisply. 'But today I have a lot to . . .'

'You certainly did.' She could almost see the gleam in the grey eyes. 'Well, I'm so glad you enjoyed it, because so did I, and I wondered if we might repeat the engagement some time? I was thinking of asking a few people round to my place. It may surprise you to hear that I'm not a bad cook, once I get going.'

'They do say the greatest chefs are male,' she countered stiffly. 'It's a nice thought, Dai, but I'm afraid it can't happen for a while yet, because I'm about to go away.'

There was a moment's surprised silence. 'You didn't mention it.' She noted with an odd satisfaction that he sounded distinctly put out.

'Didn't I? Well, I expect I thought it wasn't really anything to do with you.'

'Going anywhere nice?' His tone was sharp now, hard-edged.

'Oh yes—very nice,' she assured him with bland enthusiasm. 'Just a week's holiday. But I really need it.'

'Going all by yourself?' Did his careless tone conceal a note of discomfiture, or was it her imagination?

'No, I won't be alone. I'm not very keen on taking holidays on my own,' she told him cryptically.

'Thanks a bundle for that informative answer.' Sarcasm dripped from his words. 'That really puts me in the picture.'

'But, Dai,' she pointed out evenly, 'it's not your picture—it's mine. When I get back, perhaps we can arrange something—I like the idea of a party at your flat. Who else would be there?'

Only slightly mollified, he retrieved his brisk confidence. 'I thought I'd ask Sam and Martha Goldman. Or would that be too much of a busman's treat for you?'

'Not at all. They're both lovely. It would be fine.'

'And I dare say it would please you if I included friend Gillow as well?' he suggested heavily.

Her reply was cool and inscrutable. 'The firm would certainly be well-represented if you did. Why not ask Michele as well, and we can set up a temporary office?'

'Very droll, Mrs B. I suppose,' he went on smoothly, as if it was entirely relevant, 'this impending trip of yours doesn't happen to be a working holiday, incorporating Gillow among those present?'

She was glad he couldn't see the smile which twitched a corner of her mouth. 'Dai,' she said firmly, 'I don't see what it has to do with you where I'm going—or who with, for that matter. But since it's obviously of profound importance to you—I'm not going with Brian. As it happens, I shall be with my family. All right? Permission granted?'

'Not important, Gina—just a passing thought.' Having elicited this crucial chunk of information, he shrugged it off as if it was the last thing on earth he could be bothered with. 'Well, have a good time.'

'Thank you; I intend to. And now, if you'll excuse me . . .'

'Just one more thing. I did have a professional query to raise with you. This wasn't entirely a social call.'

'Fire away.' Picking up her pen, she began doodling on her notebook—a habit she frequently indulged in during long 'phone conversations.

'About that case.'

'Which one?' As if she didn't know. 'You're representing several of our clients at the moment, I believe.'

'You know very well which case, Gina. The one we were both so careful not to mention the other night. The one,' he elaborated, in case she had missed the point, 'I'm not taking.'

'What about it?'

'Am I still not taking it?'

'Not if I have anything to do with it, Dai.'

'I haven't earned a reprieve? You won't grant remission for good behaviour?'

Gina put down the pen and sat up, squaring her shoulders. His persistence over this relatively trivial matter was quite ludicrous, she reflected. 'Nothing's changed—the way you think, the way I think—the way we . . . clash on this subject. You said nothing the other evening which altered what you'd said before—except perhaps to reinforce it. Once I make up my mind, Dai, I can be as stubborn as the next . . .' she grinned, 'person. Even if the next person happens to be you.'

'You can say that again,' he muttered, clearly annoyed. Then he brushed the whole matter aside. 'Okay, Gina—have it your own way. Just thought I'd let you know the offer stands.'

'Thanks, Dai, but I don't think I'll be changing my . . .'

'When does it come up, anyway?' he interrupted, his tone cool.

'Not till January; so I've got plenty of time to brief anyone I like.'

'And who do you like?' he enquired, nonchalant.

'I thought I'd wait till John Slade gets back from the States—Sam says he's due before that. He always does these things exceptionally well,' she remarked wickedly.

'I'm sure he does.' The retort was curt. 'Well, I must be off and leave you to your preparations. I'll be in touch when you come back. And Gina,' he added, before she could say anything.

'Yes, Dai?'

'Thanks again for your—company. It really was most . . . stimulating.' The pitch of his voice had dropped: soft, low, intimate, it succeeded by some alchemy in by-passing her mind, forcing a path direct to her body.

'Not at all.' She fought to keep a sudden huskiness from her own voice. 'Thank *you*.'

'Till soon, then?'

'Goodbye, Dai.'

' 'Bye, Gina. Take care of yourself.'

After he had rung off, she stared at the empty receiver for a full minute—smooth brow furrowed, gold-brown eyes troubled. The more contact she had with the man, the more enigmatic he became. His physical effect on her was devastating, there was no point in denying that to herself any longer; but that, on its own, hardly constituted an adequate basis for a mature relationship. For the umpteenth time that week she delivered herself a stern lecture on the subject; and for the umpteenth time she paid very little attention to it.

A few hours later, on her way out of the office, she put

her head round Sam's door. 'I'm off now, Sam. I'll see you a week on Monday.'

His round face emerged from behind the mountain of paper on his desk—a jungle among which he could usually, by some magical process, locate almost any single item he wanted. 'Have a great time, Gina. Get a good rest. Pity about the weather—maybe it won't last all week.'

'Oh, I don't really mind, as long as I have a break. You know where I am if there are any emergencies.'

'I'm sure Brian and I can cope with any. Have you see him, by the way? He seemed a bit agitated early this morning—said he wanted to catch you before you go.'

'No.' Come to think of it, she'd seen little of Brian all week. He'd been in Court much of the time; and apart from his routine invitation, and her routine refusal, they'd exchanged few words. Even when they had, her mind had been somewhat occupied elsewhere. 'He isn't back yet. I'll give him a ring tonight, to say goodbye.'

'Yes, do that.' Sam's dark eyes rested on her thoughtfully. 'I get the impression he'd appreciate it. Not that it's any of my business, Gina,' he assured her hastily, 'but you're both my respected friends, as well as valued colleagues, and I wouldn't like you to . . .'

Gina came right into the room, closing the door behind her. 'Don't worry, Sam. I think Brian and I understand each other. We're just good friends, really.' They exchanged wry grins at the meaningless cliché. 'You know what I mean.'

'I know what you mean. I'm not sure Brian does.'

'Has Martha been talking to you again?' she demanded suspiciously. Sam's wife was well-known for her dabblings in amateur psychiatry.

'Martha,' he replied, smiling fondly, 'is always talking to me. Quite often I even listen. But no, on this occasion I've been observing Brian and working it out for myself. It isn't very difficult, Gina.'

'No, well . . .' She looked away, faintly embarrassed. 'I'll 'phone him. Now I'd better be off, Sam, if you . . .'

'One other thing. Won't keep you a minute. My mole informs me you received a call from the illustrious Mr Rees today.'

'I wasn't too pleased with that mole for putting him through without announcing him first, either,' Gina recalled grimly. 'I must have words with her about it.'

'She didn't mean any harm. And Dai can be very persuasive. That's what makes him such a wow in Court. He's going from strength to strength, you know. Not a single failure behind him since he hit London, I gather.'

'Oh, really? How nice for him. Well, Sam, I ought to be off—I've got a million things to do.'

'Did he 'phone about anything in particular?' Sam was gazing at her now with barely-disguised curiosity. 'Or would you rather I kept my big nose out of it?'

'Good lord, no—anyway, you've got every right to know, if he 'phones me at work. He wanted to make sure I hadn't changed my mind about that Haines case, that's all. He seems rather keen to do it, for obscure reasons best known to himself.' She found that she was studying her left shoe with rapt attention.

'Enjoys a challenge, I expect,' Sam speculated— hitting on several home truths at once, if he had but known it. 'And had you—changed your mind, I mean?'

'You're as bad as he is.' Suddenly tired, Gina leaned against the door. 'No, I haven't. Why should I?'

'No reason; I just wondered. So, you still want to wait and brief John when he gets back?'

'Why not?' She looked sharply up into Sam's face. 'You want Dai to do it, too, don't you?' It was more than a statement: it was an accusation. If she'd had any tendency to paranoia, she'd have suspected they were in this together.

'I didn't say that. But he really does seem to be on a

winning streak. Some potent combination of—I don't know—charisma and sheer intellectual power, I suppose. Have you seen him in action yet?'

'No.' Her tone indicated that she had better ways of passing her time.

'Well, you should; it's a revelation. He's getting some quite big cases thrown at him now; his name is beginning to be bandied about in the press. Apparently he'd already carved out quite a reputation for himself in Cardiff before he made the trek East—looks like repeating that process here.'

'So,' she said shrewdly, 'you think we should grab him for our paltry little theft cases while he's still got the time and inclination to accept them—and before his fees are too astronomical for our humble customers?'

'Something like that. But it's up to you, of course.'

'Well, if this one's up to me, I'll stick by my decision, if it's all the same to you, Sam. Get him on to as many of our other cases as you like. I'd prefer to do this one my way.'

'He really did get your dander up, didn't he?' Sam's eyes were twinkling now.

'You could say so.' With deliberate care, she masked her expression.

'Well, I mustn't keep you.' He shuffled a few papers together in a vague token of efficiency. 'Enjoy yourself. Give my regards to your parents—and don't forget to ring Brian.'

As it turned out there was no need to ring Brian. At nine o'clock, when Gina had finished her packing and was enjoying a well-earned rest, sipping a small sherry and composing a note to the milkman, he materialised at the front door.

'Brian! I was just about to 'phone you. Come in.'

She stood invitingly aside; but he stayed on the threshold, staring at her with an intensity which she barely recognised. There was a fierce, almost desperate quality in the light blue eyes which drilled into hers. His normally pale skin was flushed; his narrow shoulders, beneath the serviceable grey suit, were hunched. When he spoke, his voice was hoarse, the words chosen with careful politeness. 'Good evening, Gina. Not disturbing you, I hope?'

'Not at all.' She leaned closer, puzzled. 'Have you been drinking, Brian?' He had: she could smell the whisky on his breath. 'That's not like you.'

'What's like me, then, Gina?' He flung the sharp question at her; she stepped back in surprise, one hand still clutching the door. 'Do you really know?'

'You'd better come in, Brian.' She rubbed her eyes wearily. 'I can see this isn't going to be the kind of conversation one holds on the doorstep.'

He pushed the door open and walked past her without ceremony—without the self-effacing tact she knew so well. He made straight for her sitting-room and looked around it, as if satisfying himself that she was alone. Then he turned to face her. 'Ready for your holiday?' The wooden courtesy was back again now.

'Yes thank you, Brian. Won't you sit down?' She waved a hand towards the cord-covered, dark-brown chairs. He was slight, but he was tall; and if he was going to be in such a strange mood, she'd rather he wasn't towering over her.

But he merely continued to peruse her with that peculiar, penetrating stare. 'No thanks, I'd rather stand.'

'Coffee, then? Or another drink?' She moved past him, making for her drinks cabinet in the corner.

'No thanks, Gina. As you so accurately observed, I've had a few already. Dutch courage,' he explained disarmingly. 'Fortification.'

'Surely,' she forced her tone into its lightest pitch, 'you don't need to fortify yourself just to call on me? I'm only going away for a little over a week.'

'I haven't come to chat—nor to say goodbye for a week.' There was something new in his voice now—

something oddly dry and mechanical. 'I want to talk to you.'

'Talk away, then.' Gina hoped she was disguising her growing panic. She had never seen Brian in this mood before, and she wasn't at all sure she liked it. 'Are you sure you wouldn't rather sit down?'

'I'll say what I came to say, standing up.' He took one step in her direction; involuntarily she backed away, colliding with the oak sideboard and knocking over a tall vase of dried teazles. 'What's the matter?' he sneered. 'Not frightened of me, surely? Not dear, harmless old Brian?'

'I'm not sure what to feel,' she admitted, holding on to the sideboard for support. 'Perhaps you'd better explain why you're here—what you want.'

'If it's not clear what I want by now, Gina, it never will be.' He came another step nearer. From here he could easily have reached out and grabbed her, but he simply stood, breathing heavily as he allowed his hungry gaze to ravage her face and body. There was no room for doubt, at that moment, about what he wanted.

Gina struggled to calm her raw nerves. In a week full of challenges, this was one she had least expected. 'Brian . . . has something happened? Try and tell me what's—what's going on.'

His laugh was hollow, brittle—unnerving. 'I should tell *you* what's going on? I was rather hoping you might be able to tell *me*!'

'I don't know what you mean,' she hedged; though she was beginning to guess.

'Come on, Gina. Don't play games with me. You've been playing with me—using me—for two years. Isn't it long enough? I've held on patiently—waited for you . . . waited till you'd got over the trauma of your marriage . . . till you felt ready. I've loved you all that time, and I've held back, not wanting to rush you. And now . . .'

'Now?' she echoed. She supposed there were no

shocks in all that. If she was completely honest with herself, she had known it all along—but she had hoped it could be left submerged, comfortably buried under an unruffled surface. A vain hope, she understood suddenly; and cruel, in a way. 'What now?'

'I saw you, after you'd disappeared with that—that Rees fellow at Jackie's party. I saw you, Gina, and I'm not a fool. I may not cut much of a dash, but I wasn't born yesterday—and I know you. I saw your face later, too, when you talked about him in the pub. I know what's going on.'

'Nothing's . . . going on, Brian.' She repeated it, to make it sound more convincing. 'Nothing; honestly.'

'Well, if it isn't yet,' he rasped, 'you'd like it to be.'

She held out her hands to him, appealing. 'What can I say, Brian? What can I do to reassure you? Dai Rees and I . . . there's a certain electricity between us, I'll admit that—when we ever stop arguing. I hardly know the man, anyway. Compared to him, you're an old and valued friend . . .'

'*An old and valued friend*,' he mimicked unkindly. 'Dull, dependable—is that it? Unexceptionable, unexciting?'

'You know what I mean.' She groped desperately for words that might soothe him. 'I've only just met Dai. You're a—a part of my life. He's . . .'

'What, Gina? He's what?' His hands reached for her now, bony fingers harsh on her shoulders. 'Whatever he is, it's something I'm not, and never will be—even if you've only just met him. Aren't I right?' His grip tightened.

She stared, aghast at this unexpected complication. 'What do you want, Brian?' she whispered, drymouthed. 'How can I make you believe . . .?'

'Only one way, Gina. Like this.' He pulled her roughly towards him; and then his mouth was assaulting hers. She allowed herself to go limp, neither resisting nor responding as the kiss ground on . . . and on. He had never inspired much feeling in her, one

way or the other: there was no revulsion, but there was
no spark, either. His touch—his presence—did
nothing to her, for her, at all; that was exactly what
made their relationship so welcome, so safe. Or had
been, at least, up to this point. Too late, she
understood how potentially explosive it had been; how
misguided she had been, expecting to prolong it
indefinitely.

When he finally released her, red and gasping for
breath, she had never known him so aroused. It had
been convenient to believe that the Brian she knew
was barely capable of such passion. Acute shame
mingled with her pity and anxiety. It was true: she had
used him; she had been deeply unfair.

His hands left her shoulders now, dropping
uselessly to his sides; but his stare was no less intense.
'Marry me, Gina,' he entreated hoarsely. 'Your
divorce would be no more than a formality now. Get
one—and marry me—please.'

Her head swam. So—there was no further room for
compromise. He was forcing the issue to a head,
whether she liked it or not. A few months ago, she
might even have considered his ragged proposal. Even
if one essential ingredient of a complete marriage was
missing—on her side, at least she might have opted
for the cosy stability, the security of the rest . . . and
they were good friends, did get on well . . . but
now . . .

What was the difference now? The answer was a
searing flash, scorching her brain, incontrovertible,
unarguable: the truth, the whole truth and nothing but
the truth. Since her recent contacts with Dai, she
couldn't fool herself—or Brian—any longer. There
was no way she could honestly make a match based on
mental compatibility alone—any more than one based
entirely on desire.

She almost laughed outright. Fuse Dai and Brian
together—roll them up into a single unit—and you
might have the perfect mate. Taken separately, there

was no future for her with either of them as anything more than occasional company. They fulfilled separate parts of her nature—doomed to stay separate, it seemed, for ever.

Now that Brian's pent-up emotions had been let out, he was calmer, watching as she turned her back on him and walked slowly to the other end of the room. There, she stood for a full minute in silence before swinging round to confront him again.

'I can't, Brian. I can't marry you. It wouldn't be fair.'

His eyes were beseeching, but his frame had relaxed. 'Don't you love me at all?'

'I'm very fond of you. There's no one I'm fonder of ... but I'm not in love with you. I'm not,' she repeated emphatically—knowing at last that it was kinder to be cruel. 'And I can't pretend to be. You do know that really, don't you?'

'I know you've never even pretended to find me—attractive, in that way. But I thought you were just guarding yourself, after ... If you were willing to give it a try, Gina, I'm sure we could work it out together. We've got so much going for us—I'm on my own, and you're ... you and Toby ...'

'I shall never marry,' she declared forcefully, 'just to provide Toby with a father. We've managed all right so far, and we'll go on managing.'

'I didn't mean to imply ... I know you can manage, Gina. I don't know anyone who manages as well as you do. It's me who can't manage without you.' His voice broke; his face crumpled. Compassion almost persuaded her to give in; but it was no substitute—she reminded herself in the nick of time—for passion.

'No, Brian. I'm sorry. I'm truly, deeply sorry. Please believe that I like and respect you enormously, and if this means we can't go on being friends and seeing each other—I shall be genuinely sad. Something very important will go out of my life. But I've kept you on a string long enough.' She lifted her head proudly. 'I won't delude either of us into thinking it's been anything it hasn't—not any more.' *Not now*, her mind added. *Now that I've sampled the other thing.*

His fierce determination had run its course, and now he was an unhappy, rather pathetic reflection of the man who had arrived at the flat half an hour earlier. He sank into an armchair, sandy head in hands. 'Oh Gina,' he mumbled. 'What must you think of me? What have I done?'

She came up to him and laid a gentle hand on his shoulder. 'Only been honest, Brian. That can only be good.' She stooped to look into his face. 'As far as I'm concerned we can go on as before—still be friends.' There was an urgency behind the soothing words. 'It would make things at work impossible if we couldn't. One of us would have to leave the firm—and I don't think either of us wants that?'

He shook his head, still unable to meet her eyes. 'I should have waited—if I'd given you longer ... eventually you might have come round to me.'

'I don't think so, Brian. Not in the way you want me to.' Her quiet firmness compelled him to accept the truth at last, however painful.

His reddened eyes lifted to stare into hers. 'Just tell me this, Gina—has your reaction to my ... proposal got anything—anything at all—to do with Dai Rees?'

The directness of the question shocked her; she felt colour leaping to her face. 'I ...'

In his rueful affection, he almost smiled. 'Don't say any more. It's written all over you. I was a fool to think I could compete with a man like that. If only I'd got myself worked up to ask you months ago!' He shrugged; now that the scene was over, she began to suspect he had known its outcome all along—accepted it, at some level of him, already.

'But Brian—you've got it all wrong about Dai. It's not like that at all. I've only been out with him once.' It was her turn to become agitated, to pace the room, while he sat still, regarding her steadily.

'You may not realise it yet, Gina; but as I said, I'm not a fool and I know you very well.' He sighed deeply, pushing back a lock of fair hair. 'No use asking what's he got that I haven't, is it?'

She paused by his chair, looking down at him. 'You might also ask,' she pointed out, 'what you've got that he hasn't? Because believe me, there's plenty. There's patience and tolerance, and . . .'

'Plenty there may be,' he conceded, 'but it's that other bit that matters, in the end.' He did smile then, weakly. 'Don't worry, Gina. I love you, and I expect I always will; but I've got it off my chest now, as I should have had the guts to do a long time ago.' He stood up. 'And now that we know where we stand, I'll leave you to your packing.'

She had to admire his philosophical stoicism. 'Not even a cup of coffee first?'

'No thanks. And don't worry—when you get back, things will be just as they've always been. I won't make it difficult for you. Now that I've proved what I've always really suspected, perhaps I can begin to be . . . realistic about you.'

'You'll find someone else, Brian. I know you will. Whoever they are will be very lucky,' she added sincerely.

'At this moment, I doubt it very much; but I'm prepared to believe anything's possible.' He smiled again; a smile which projected a deep weariness. 'Goodbye, Gina.'

Seeing him to the door, she didn't insult him with her usual light, sisterly peck on the cheek. They looked at each other across the hall, a new distance and yet a new understanding between them. 'Goodbye, Brian.'

'Have a lovely time at your parents'. Return refreshed.'

'I'll try,' she said, closing the door behind him.

Driving north and west next morning in drizzle and

mist, she went through the motions competently enough; but her mind was in a turmoil the whole way, as it had been much of the long night. What strange confluence of planets was manipulating her destiny just now; what forces were in action, exposing her safe, air-tight little world—tearing her ostrich-like head from the ground?

First Dai Rees had barged into her life to ride rough-shod over ideas and emotions alike—pulverising the intellectual cocoon she had methodically built up around herself. Then—driven out of his natural torpor by that same catalyst—her kind, stable, reliable friend Brian had erupted into a near-stranger, dragging new sensations of alarm and guilt in his wake.

One thing was quite obvious: she hadn't been organising her life as successfully as she'd thought, all this time. Too much had been hidden away; honesty had been sacrificed to outer serenity. As a result, she'd come dangerously close to losing Brian altogether ... and the challenge presented by Dai was almost too terrifying, and yet too enticing, to contemplate.

It was a pale, exhausted Gina who finally gained the haven of the stone-built village to be greeted by her loving parents and reunited with her ecstatic son. Toby noticed nothing out of the ordinary, and was far too busy in any case, regaling her with every possible detail of his fortnight's activities. If her parents wondered why their only daughter seemed tense and preoccupied during her stay, they were too tactful to say so. They offered wordless, devoted support as they always had; and she knew she could talk to them about it if she wanted to.

But the peace of the place was a balm to her shredded nerve-endings, and a few days of rest and relaxation repaired the worst of the damage. For all her sensitivity, Gina was a resilient person—though not as tough as she liked to think she was. By the time the end of the week approached, she found herself quite calm at the prospect of returning to the fray.

One thing she had now learned, at least: there was absolutely no point in running away. Sooner or later you were bound to catch up with yourself.

CHAPTER EIGHT

DURING the next few weeks Gina took two significant steps: she gave up wearing her wedding ring; and she set divorce proceedings in action at last.

Apart from these major decisions, she kept her head well down, burying herself in hard work. Work, and Toby: these were her realities. In them she sought refuge from the new twists of fate which threatened to shatter her emotional stability. If she had been an ostrich for years, she had been a perfectly contented one; and she wasn't about to have her head plucked from its sandy hiding place without a struggle.

Brian's mood at the office was detached, almost formal. He was amicable enough, but he had pointedly given up asking her out. If she looked at him carefully, the signs of pain were there about the eyes, the line of his mouth—but Gina knew him much better than most people. Outwardly, nothing had changed. Inwardly, she had the feeling he'd get over it surprisingly soon.

Dai continued to make his presence in her life felt, whether she welcomed it or not. His voice vibrated across the telephone wires regularly, issuing cheerful invitations. He appeared totally undaunted by her repeated refusals, and just kept trying; and eventually his persistence paid off. On two occasions—when she reckoned his proposed activities were suitably safe and public—Gina accepted.

The first time, they went to the theatre: a new play at the Aldwych. Once again he disarmed her by proving to be a relaxed, charming companion. Geared up as she was to fight him off, she found her armour quite unnecessary; apparently without effort, he created an atmosphere between them which contrived to be intimate and yet discreet. He touched her only when politeness made it inevitable; and somehow his very restraint emphasised the brutal fact that, for Gina, his proximity alone was exciting. She began to ask herself whether she had reacted too strongly to those earlier moments of contact. Perhaps she had even imagined his direct, explicit statement of intent?

All the same she declined his suggestion of supper afterwards, and as soon as they drew up outside her flat she bolted from the car like a rabbit from a gun, muttering excuses about babysitters—leaving him sitting at the wheel, staring across at her with an expression of wry amusement. She wasn't taking any chances.

The second time, he took her to a Promenade concert at the Albert Hall. She had always enjoyed classical music, but there was something special about the Proms in their ornate Gothic setting—the vast dome, the cavernous auditorium, the eccentric acoustic, the good-humoured cheering from the standing audience at the front. It was a light-hearted event, and its mood reached out to include them both as the lyrical strains of Mozart and Beethoven washed over them.

When the Lancia pulled up at her door, she made to jump out again; but he laid a firm hand on her arm as she fumbled for the handle. 'Gina.' His voice was low and gentle. 'I won't bite. There's no need to flee my presence as if I were a serious threat to life and limb. It's not good for my ego,' he added satirically.

A serious threat—that probably summed it up quite accurately, Gina's mind warned; but she turned reluctantly to face him. 'I'd hate to bruise your no doubt sensitive ego,' she retorted, 'but it's just that I promised to be in by . . .'

'It's not eleven yet,' he pointed out. 'I'm sure they'll wait a minute, whoever they are. Perhaps I can drive them home?' he suggested, with only the faintest gleam in his eye.

'That won't be necessary. Tracey lives just down

the road—and she's only seventeen, so . . .'

'So you'd prefer not to entrust her to my dubious care?' he taunted.

'I was about to explain,' she went on coldly, 'that her father normally walks up here to see her home. So there's no need—thanks all the same.'

'Well, I won't keep you from her a moment. I wanted to tell you—I've fixed up that evening at my place—the one we mentioned before you went away. Sam and Martha will definitely be there. I want to make sure you're free too.'

It sounded innocuous enough, but Gina's guard stiffened. 'When?'

'Two weeks Saturday suit you?'

She thought carefully. 'I'm free then—but I'll have to check whether Jackie can have Toby. It's more difficult to find babysitters on Saturday nights, so I usually leave him with her. She may be going out herself. I'll let you know.'

That gave her a let-out clause, without seeming downright offensive. Dai was studying her closely. 'In principle, then, you're not averse to the idea?'

She stared straight ahead. 'If the Goldmans are coming, it should be very pleasant. I always like seeing them.'

'You consider them suitable chaperons?' She could feel the impact as his gaze played mockingly on her profile.

'I think they'll be lively company,' she amended primly. 'Thanks for the invitation, Dai.' She flicked a glance at him. 'I'm surprised you can fit in culinary activity among all your many other major enterprises.'

'I told you before, I'm remarkably proficient in the kitchen—and I enjoy anything I'm good at,' he drawled. 'I might even wear my frilly apron over my Male Chauvinist Pig tie,' he mused, his gaze still on her face.

'That should be a sight for sore eyes. Now, Dai, it's been a lovely evening, but I must . . .'

'Funny,' he interrupted, as if she hadn't spoken. 'I

bumped into Gillow in Holborn the other day—asked
if he'd like to be included in this event, thinking he'd
leap at the chance if you were going to be there—but it
appears he's otherwise engaged.'

'Brian has his own life to lead.' She forced the
stiffness from her lips and tone. 'We see plenty of each
other at work.'

'Of course, of course,' he soothed. 'No need to get
ruffled.'

'I am not in the least ruffled—but I've got to go in
now. Good night, Dai—and thanks.' She opened her
door and got out.

'Good night, Gina.' This time, the car was gone by
the time she reached her front steps—leaving nothing
but a small cloud of exhaust fumes hanging on the
misty autumn air.

October was well under way. Toby had settled
happily into his new class at school. Office routine
was comfortingly regular. Paperwork mounted up in
stacks; cases were won and lost; houses bought and
sold; clients came and went. Gina telephoned Peggy
Haines to explain that her hearing at the Crown
Court had been fixed for the middle of January, and
that she would be briefing a suitable Counsel just as
soon as he returned from a trip to America in
December.

'Not before that?' Peggy sounded doubtful.

'Don't worry—that leaves us plenty of time. It only
takes them a day or two to assimilate all the
information. Even if they want to meet you, a week's
notice is good enough.'

'I'll never get through the waiting,' Peggy moaned.
'Three months! It's like a great big axe hanging over
my head. I never forget about it, Mrs Barton, not for a
moment. Jim doesn't say much but I know he thinks
about it too. The kids are really sweet, but . . .'

'It'll pass quicker than you think,' Gina encouraged her. 'Some people have to wait much

longer than that, Mrs Haines—you've been quite lucky really.'

'Well, I just hope it's all worth it in the end,' sighed Peggy despondently.

So do I, Gina's mind endorsed grimly; but her calmest voice said: 'Of course it will be. You're doing the right thing—trust me.'

'So—when does this shoplifting case of yours come up again?' Martha Goldman eased her short, comfortable form further into the corner of one of Dai Rees's luxuriously deep, plump olive-green sofas. Her quick brown eyes scrutinised Gina—sitting at the opposite corner—over the top of her Martini.

Gina sipped her gin and tonic, savouring its sweet-and-bitter taste through the ice and lemon. 'Mid-January.' She wished this subject wouldn't keep cropping up. Glancing round anxiously, she relaxed a little: Dai was nowhere to be seen—probably busy in the gleaming, all-mod-cons kitchen he had proudly exhibited to them as they arrived, concocting whatever delicacies they were about to receive. In the domestic domain, as everywhere else, he was all creative self-assurance.

'One hardly knows whether to respect a man like this, or resent him,' Sam had murmured in her ear as the two of them stood gazing through vast expanses of picture window on to a green-and-grey tableau of London. Grateful for his endearing candour, Gina had flashed a responsive grin at him.

'It's a fine flat, though.' Her glance had travelled wistfully across the spacious room with its plush cream wall-to-wall Wilton, heavy velvet drapes, furniture redolent of taste and comfort; its walls enhanced with an unusual assortment of original paintings, both classical and modern. 'And what about this view!'

'He's got the taste to go with the status, I'll give him that,' Sam had commented—casting her a quizzical look, just as the man himself had returned with their drinks.

'Gina doesn't want to talk about that case tonight, Martha,' Sam reproached his wife now, from the enfolding depths of an armchair which almost drowned him. 'It's her night off. Anyway she has good reason to prefer not to discuss it here—haven't you, Gina?'

'Oh, I know all about that,' Martha declared airily. 'It's all right, Sam—I hope I've got enough tact to keep off that subject once Dai gets back.'

'I hope you have, too,' he agreed drily.

Martha ignored his sarcasm. 'That poor woman. When Sam told me the story, I was so sorry for her. I didn't blame you, Gina, for having a go at defending her yourself. But you're doing the best thing now—John Slade's the right man for the job.'

'I'm glad you think so,' Gina smiled gratefully at this unexpected support.

'Though mind you,' Martha continued archly, 'you could have done a whole lot worse than our host, too.' She helped herself to a stuffed olive from a glass bowl.

'He's doing well altogether, I believe.' Gina seized on the shift of topic with some relief. Sam was right: she didn't particularly want to air it this evening.

'Doing well! He's making headlines, my dear. Not just in the legal journals—in the nationals as well. Did you see the article in *The Times* yesterday about that tricky libel suit he won for a TV scriptwriter? Apparently he engineered this amazing twist . . .'

'What about the film star he's just got off a serious drug charge,' Sam contributed. 'What's her name—you know—glamorous American type—anyway, no one thought she stood a chance but he found a small crack in the prosecution's evidence and blew it open a mile wide. Exploited it brilliantly. After that, they didn't have a leg to stand on.'

Martha leaned forwards in her enthusiasm. 'The one that interests me is this latest rape case. You must know about that one, Gina?'

Gina, who hadn't heard about any of them, shook her head. She had the distinct impression she was about to be told. 'Well, he's representing this guy,' Sam began to explain laboriously, 'who's accused of raping a very young girl . . .'

'*Very* young,' Martha underlined darkly. 'Hardly any older than our Charlotte. Disgusting.'

'We don't know that he actually did it, Martha,' Sam reminded her. 'Anyhow, it seems he claims she was leading him on—and she denies it—and then he says nothing really happened, despite what she says. The point is, he's some kind of big-shot—a Member of the House of Lords or something . . .'

'Related to Royalty?' Martha speculated hopefully.

'Possibly some minor Earl or other,' Sam recalled vaguely. 'Anyway . . .'

'Or was it just that he owned a corgi?' The miracle-worker himself had unobtrusively arrived in the doorway behind them. Three heads turned in unison to meet their host's sardonic gaze. He lounged on the doorframe, a powerful figure in slim brown cord jeans and tan linen overshirt, hands in pockets.

'We were just telling Gina about this rape case you've got yourself on to,' Martha informed him brightly.

'So I gathered.' His tone made it clear that the matter was, as far as he was concerned, *sub judice* for the evening. 'Well, folks, I've removed my apron—all is prepared—will you do me the honour of repairing to the dining room for a spot of supper?'

Seldom had Gina been more glad of an excuse to drop a subject. Although it held a certain sordid fascination, she found herself strangely unwilling to hear the details. If Dai chose to defend probable—or even possible—rapists, however aristocratically connected, that was his business; but she'd rather know as little about it as strictly necessary.

She stood up—and was suddenly acutely conscious of three pairs of eyes taking in the details of her Indian cotton suit—the full skirt swirling to her trim calves, the close-fitting waistcoat accentuating her softly generous shape. Its brown print toned with the plain fawn blouse underneath—front tucks rising to a high, demure neckline; full sleeves gathered into tight cuffs.

Sam, as usual, said exactly what he thought. 'You look delicious tonight, Gina. Good enough to eat.'

'You do,' agreed Martha good-naturedly. 'That's a lovely suit.'

'Doesn't she?' Dai's voice was low, his grey eyes ranging over every crease, every curve. 'I can only hope I've made enough food so that we aren't tempted.' With this cryptic comment, he led them across the wide hallway and into the dining room.

'This is a fantastic flat,' Martha enthused, settling herself into the chair her husband held out for her. 'You were lucky to find it.'

'Not so much of the lucky,' Dai pushed Gina's chair in behind her—leaving a frisson where his fingertips rested briefly on her shoulders. 'I went about it in a highly methodical manner. As soon as I knew I was heading for London, I reconnoitred the most desirable areas, got in touch with the best estate agents and told them to find me something with two bedrooms, in a reasonably modern block, and with a great outlook. When they heard my price range,' he recalled complacently, 'they soon did.'

'Isn't it rather big for one person?' Beneath the coy question, Gina knew Martha was remembering their guided tour of the place earlier. Against her better judgment, her own mind returned to the adequate second bedroom, the guest bathroom, the bright master-suite with its king-sized bed under a woven Spanish bedspread.

'I like to have space.' Dai's expression was blandly masked. 'Now, who likes avocado with prawns?'

'Lovely,' said Gina. Was she doomed to spend the evening attempting to divert uncomfortable topics? 'One of my favourites.'

But Sam wasn't to be so easily deflected. 'I bet you don't always have it to yourself, eh, Dai?' His wink was broad and blatant. 'A chap has to relax sometimes—especially when he's as hard-working as you are.'

'Sam!' Martha's raised eyebrows made a pretence of disapproval—but her eager brown eyes gave her own curiosity away. 'I can't take him anywhere, Dai—take no notice of him.'

'Oh, I shan't—don't worry, Martha.' Dai grinned—the perfect host, oiling the wheels, neither giving nor taking offence. 'I'm no monk, if that's what you're getting at, Sam. On the other hand, I do like to keep my private self private, on the whole.' There was just the hint of a crisp warning at the edge of his tone.

Sam nodded gravely. 'Naturally—that's your prerogative. Forgive the voyeuristic fantasies of a happily married man,' he pleaded humbly, digging into his avocado.

'Sam!' complained Martha again, as she attacked her own prawns; but her glare held more affection than conviction.

'Nothing to forgive. You are entitled to your speculations.' Still smiling, Dai refilled their glasses with chilled Liebfraumilch—light, tangy, refreshing.

Gina was busying herself scooping out the last tender flesh of her avocado. The conversation this evening seemed determined to hit embarrassing personal notes; and it had just come to her, with a jarring shock, that she never had pursued her own probings into Dai's past. He had been so cagey, that first time, that she'd hardly liked to retrace such touchy territory. Obviously he specialised in keeping his private life well under wraps—doubtless in direct proportion to the publicity his professional activities received.

'Okay, people. And for my next trick . . .' With a dramatic flourish, Dai lifted the lid of a silver chafing-dish to reveal eight long skewers threaded with grilled chunks of lamb, garnished with tomatoes and green peppers.

'Kebabs! How marvellous!' Martha was overcome with admiration. 'Where did you pick up all these domestic skills, Dai? You're a man of many parts, that's for sure.' She watched eagerly as Dai eased the meat on to plates with a fork.

'I believe anything's worth doing well, if it's worth doing at all. Actually I enjoy cooking, but I don't often give myself the chance to do it properly. That's why it's good to have friends round to share it, once in a while.'

'You can have us round any time.' Sam helped himself to fluffy rice.

But Martha wasn't letting him off the hook so easily. 'You hear that, Sam? This man's a magician in the kitchen as well as in Court. Who says cooking's a female occupation? There's nothing female,' she added archly, 'about Dai.'

'So what are you shouting about, woman?' Sam was quite unconcerned. 'Aren't my scrambled eggs the toast of Islington?'

Gina laughed as she took some crisp mixed salad from a wooden bowl. 'They're very good; I've tasted them.'

Martha pulled a face at her. 'Whose side are you on, anyway?' she grumbled. 'He's quite cocky enough without support from our team.'

'I wasn't aware,' Dai remarked, drawing the cork smoothly from a bottle of Burgundy, 'that we were in the midst of a battle.'

'Come now, Dai.' Sam held out his glass to be filled. 'Where opposite sexes are gathered together, surely you always are?'

'I'm sure Mrs Barton would agree with you there.' Dai leaned towards Gina to pour the glowing red wine into her glass, his grey eyes sparkling.

'Not at all,' she denied vehemently, sipping it. It was dry and rich and wonderfully warming. 'On the contrary, I think it's most unnecessary, all the fighting that goes on. We should all . . .'

'Live together in peace and harmony? How dull!' he mocked.

'Not much chance of that, with Martha around,' observed Sam gloomily—defusing their momentary tension.

As they ate their main course, Dai steered the conversation adroitly on to more general matters; and by the time they reached the fresh fruit salad and cream they were all expressing equally vociferous opinions about the latest series of industrial confrontations. After what seemed a ridiculously short time, they were re-established in the lounge, relaxing over strong black coffee and brandies.

It wasn't just the good food, plentiful wine and convivial company that induced this sense of heady wellbeing in the group. Dai was as successful as a host, Gina had to admit, as he was at most other things. Sam's sardonic sentiment re-echoed round her head: *One hardly knows whether to respect a man like this, or resent him.* The more she got to know of Dai Rees, the more apt that statement was.

Regretfully, Martha stood up and stretched. 'We have to go home, Sam; we promised the sitter we wouldn't be late.'

'It's only eleven-thirty,' Dai protested. 'The night is yet young.'

'Unfortunately, so is our sitter.' Martha giggled. 'We have to keep in their good books or they won't come again. The girls are getting to be quite a handful.'

'Doesn't Charlotte look after the little ones?' Gina asked, surprised.

'Sometimes, when she hasn't got a date herself—but you know how it is, at nearly sixteen you have your own scene. The last thing you need is to be lumbered with two kid sisters. Come on, Sam.' She tapped her reluctant husband on the shoulder. 'Time to go home. Is it safe to let you drive, or do I have to do it?'

'I didn't notice you practising much abstinence with Dai's highly acceptable wine,' Sam returned. 'Anyway, I think I prefer my own driving when I've had one or two, to yours when you're stone cold sober.'

Martha wagged a finger at him. 'Wait till I get you home, sexist pig!'

'Is that a threat or a promise?' Sam rose unwillingly to his feet, grinning cheekily at his wife. Then he turned to Dai. 'It's been a great evening, Dai. Thank you so much. Can we give you a lift, Gina?' he added as an afterthought.

'She came in her own car, silly. We arrived at the same time, remember? Some women are capable of managing a vehicle, you know,' Martha reminded him scathingly. Dai flashed a mischievous glance at Gina, which she affected to ignore. 'Thanks a million, Dai.' Martha beamed at her host. 'You must come and eat with us soon. 'Bye, Gina.'

But Gina had stood up too, and was moving purposefully into the hall with them. 'I'll be off as well, I think. I'm rather tired, and it's . . .'

'Don't be silly.' Martha was outraged at such a notion. 'No need to leave so early, just because we have to. Who's minding Toby?'

'Oh, he's safely at Jackie's for the night, but I think I'll still . . .'

'Nonsense. What's the matter—afraid of being abandoned here, unchaperoned?' Sam was teasing—or was he? 'I'm sure Dai is the soul of propriety.' Gina was far from sure; but she said nothing. 'No, don't hurry off on our account, Gina. We really have got to go, but we'd hate to think we were breaking up the evening.'

What was this—some kind of conspiracy? Dai's expression was a study in self-righteous humour. He hadn't had to utter a single word: the Goldmans had done all his persuading for him. Gina subsided; the last thing she wanted to do was make an issue of it. As soon as they were safely out of the way, she was off.

With many noises of appreciation and gratitude,

they finally went. When Dai reappeared after seeing them off, Gina was standing by the mantelshelf, examining some small pieces of pottery and sculpture. She swung round as soon as he entered, ready to take her leave.

'Admiring my collection? I like good shapes—abstracts. I've picked up these over the years.' He kept his distance—now disconcertingly brisk, offhand even. 'How about one more cup of coffee for the road, as the man said? I'm going to have one anyway—and I don't suppose you'll want to stay much longer?'

The invitation seemed straightforward enough. She glanced at him searchingly: his face was quite impassive. Perhaps, she thought again, her fears had been paranoid; perhaps he had no intention, after all, of getting any closer. Perhaps she wasn't reacting in a very mature fashion.

She took a deep breath. 'All right—thanks.' An idea struck her. 'Can I help you wash up first?' It always felt safer if you were doing something practical.

His reply was uncompromising. 'No way, Gina. Guests in my home don't work for their keep. If I can cook a meal, I can clear up after it. I have no wish to shirk the more menial side of life, whatever you may think of me. Anyway,' he admitted, with a slightly lopsided grin, 'I do have a wonderful person who comes in to clean, every weekday.'

'Fair enough. I only asked,' she observed—cool, defensive.

But his warmest smile melted another layer of her armour. 'And I only answered. So—coffee coming up. Make yourself comfortable; won't be a moment.'

She sat down again, gingerly, on the edge of the couch, and picked up a magazine—one of a pile of colour supplements and weeklies lying on the coffee table. She was half-heartedly skimming a florid description of the Favourite Room of a Notable Personality when he returned, quietly closing the door behind him.

'You don't take sugar, do you?' He set the tray down on the table—efficient, businesslike, almost impersonal. His glance fell on what she was reading. 'Can't stand those pretentious articles. What the hell does it matter what their room is like? A room is just a room. You can't tell much about anyone from that.'

Her gaze drifted round the one they were in—generous, positive; organised but lived-in. 'Oh, I don't know,' she contradicted mildly.

He sat beside her, but not too close—his whole attention apparently concentrated on pouring the coffee. Its rich aroma reached out to her nostrils. His presence only inches away reached out to her other senses. Warning lights flashed dimly; but he was no threat tonight, surely, in this mood of well-bred hospitality? She made a sudden decision to trust him—after all, she could always beat a hasty retreat if things became too challenging.

They sipped their coffee in companionable silence. Cradling his cup in his left hand, he relaxed, stretching his long legs out in front of him. His right arm found its way—inadvertently, it seemed, as part of the general stretch—across the back of the sofa behind her shoulders. She froze within her reactions; but she made no move.

He smiled lazily at her. 'Enjoy the evening, Gina? Sweet, aren't they—Martha and Sam?'

'I've enjoyed it very much,' she replied truthfully, returning the smile. 'Yes, I like them both—and they're not just sweet, either. They're both very clever people. Martha was a Legal Executive, you know, before . . .'

'Yes, yes, I know. Another high-powered lady. But not,' he added, his voice dropping to that lower, more intimate note he had been studiously avoiding, 'as beautiful a one as you.'

She should have known better than to trust him—or herself, her mind pointed out acidly. 'Dai, I . . .' She shifted away from him until she was jammed up against the arm of the couch.

'Got to leave now? Remembered something urgent?'
With deliberate actions, he set his coffee cup on the
table, took hers from her hand and put it beside his.
Then he turned round to face her; and quite suddenly
his arms were pinning her back into her corner, up
against the olive-green weave of the upholstery.

It was too late. There was nothing to be done,
even if she wanted to escape. And did she? Her eyelashes dropped, shielding her eyes from his. Why
was this sense of helplessness as delicious as it was
terrifying? What was happening to her? 'No ... I
just thought . . .' she mumbled.

'You thought I'd forgotten—let you off the hook?
No chance, Gina.' His voice throbbed now with
controlled intensity; a control, it told her clearly,
which was on the point of slipping. 'I meant what I
said—there's a little matter waiting to be sorted out
between you and me, Mrs B. You can't run away from
it forever. And I'll tell you another thing.'

'What?' she whispered, allowing her glance to stray
up to his.

'Nothing is going to happen that we don't both
want—equally—and that's a promise.'

'How can you know that?' she breathed, as his
hands left the arm of the sofa to start a slow, thorough
investigation of the contours of her face—broad
fingertips acquainting themselves with the curves of
her cheeks and chin, the smooth column of her neck.
The very gentleness of him was her undoing; the other
side of the coin from that forceful dominance she had
come to expect. She tried one last time. 'The other
week, I was . . .'

'The other week,' he murmured, his fingers never
ceasing their subtle explorations, 'we were like two
kids scrabbling on the wet grass.' She wouldn't have
put it quite like that, but she let it pass. 'This time,
we're two consenting adults in a warm, comfortable,
private place; and we have all the time in the world.
Right?'

She shook her head; but she was transfixed by the steady motions of his hands, the deep timbre of his tone, the light in his eyes. It was no good pretending she was drunk, or dreaming; she was fully sober and awake—more awake than she had ever been—and she liked it. She sat perfectly still as his fingers left her neck and untied the top string of her waistcoat—and the next, and the next, until it hung open all the way down. Patiently—his expression still tender, intent— he started on the tiny buttons of her blouse.

'I thought,' he muttered, 'chastity belts went out with the dark ages.'

With care—almost with reverence—he pushed the soft material aside, revealing the last, skimpy layer of protection beneath. The simple bra was soon disposed of; and still she stayed exactly where she was, scarcely breathing, hypnotised by his understated movements.

Hands now on her bare shoulders, he stared for long, long moments at the fine, full, falling swell of her breasts. His feasting eyes seared her flesh as surely, as sharply, as any physical contact could have done. There was no disguising her body's response under that penetrating gaze. Outwardly, it hardened— rising to meet him. Inwardly, a flutter became a dull ache which spread and intensified into a profound, an intolerably fierce hunger.

Even the sound of his voice sharpened her longing. She yearned for him to touch her—but his hands were firm and motionless on her shoulders as his eyes drank her body in. 'Gina.' The tone had become strangely thick and husky. 'You're magnificent. You're the most desirable woman I've ever seen.' Gradually his head bent towards her; she closed her eyes, welcoming. 'I've never wanted any woman as much as I want you.' The words were almost lost as his mouth discovered hers—parting her lips, seeking her tongue—but still gentle, undemanding as it nibbled and tasted.

Her hands found their own way round his neck, fingers tangling in the springing vitality of his hair;

then under his shirt, revelling in the warm firmness of his skin, tracing the long, hard line of his spine. His hands clasped her head as the kiss deepened; then reached round to release the clip from her hair and unwind it so that it fell—a richly glowing curtain about her shoulders and upper arms.

Then, and only then, they moved down from her shoulders to find her breasts—cupping and shaping and stroking—square, sensitive thumbs brushing and coaxing the dark tips into scorched points of flame. Arching, straining against him Gina knew that the last dregs of spurious modesty had ebbed away as passion flooded in to to take their place.

She had a lot of catching up to do; and he was the man she was going to do it with. On both counts, he had been right. She was a grown woman—a mother—with mature needs and instincts, which had as much right to fulfilment as any other part of her nature—but which had been sadly neglected for years. And in Dai's expert hands, her body became a beautifully modulated instrument, only waiting for a great musician to bring it to life with his perfect understanding of its potential.

And now his mouth had dragged itself away from hers, his lips leaving a blazing trail down her neck and chest as they moved to take over the prolonged exploration of her breasts. His fingers had reached the zip of her skirt, and were lightly tracing the roundness of her waist, stomach and hips. The music was rising to a natural crescendo—all thought finally obliterated as Gina's mind went gladly under. Her hands sought out his body, forgetting all shame; his became hard, possessive against her supple smoothness.

The ringing doorbell was a minor irritant, an intrusion from a long way off. Deeply engrossed in each other, they ignored it. After a while it came again—sharp, shrill, insistent. 'Someone's ...' muttered Gina, struggling to sit up.

'They'll go away,' murmured Dai, against her skin.

But they did not go away. They rang again—and again, longer and louder. After that, there was a silence at last: the person, whoever it was (and who could it be, at such a late hour?) had obviously given up. Gina relaxed under Dai's spell again—only to be startled into even greater alarm by the unmistakable rattle of a key in a lock, which seemed to reverberate through the peace of the flat.

This time Dai was forced into reluctant action. With a fervent curse, he sat up, running a hand through his already dishevelled hair, staring at Gina with mingled apology and rage—the latter surely not, her confused mind shouted, aimed at her? Then he was on his feet, straightening out his shirt, striding towards the door of the room.

Gina moved swiftly, reflexively—grabbing her blouse and doing up as many buttons as her shaking fingers could manage; picking up her waistcoat from the floor; standing up to fasten the waistband of her skirt; locating her bra and stuffing it into her bag. If it hadn't been more than a little undignified, and much too sudden, the whole situation might—she reflected ruefully—have been positively comic. Her mind was regaining its usual watchfulness—wondering what nocturnal caller was the trusted holder of one of Dai's front-door keys.

She didn't have long to wonder. Even as Dai reached the door, a voice from the hall was calling his name—a female voice, tinkling and sweet. 'Dai-ee!' it trilled, coming closer. 'Are you up? Are you here?'

He opened the door just as the intruder got to it; and they confronted each other in the open doorway. 'I'm here—and I'm up, as you see,' he informed her tersely. 'But I'm not alone.'

Gina could make out the top of a silvery blonde head; then cornflower blue eyes, peering inquisitively over Dai's broad shoulder. 'Oh, I'm so sorry!' the voice exclaimed—sounding anything but. 'It's so late ... I've just got back from one of those boring business parties, and I wondered if you might still be up and feel like a bit of . . . company.' She pushed past him to take a dainty step into the room, and Gina saw her clearly for the first time: her svelte form was encased in a clinging black catsuit. Dai's eyes narrowed, but he did not prevent her. 'I can see you've already got some,' she concluded, staring openly at Gina.

Gina returned the stare. That sensation of heightened reality was slipping; she felt herself falling into a dream—or was it a nightmare? She clenched her fists, fighting to recapture some of that recent magic and mystery; but it had vanished, evaporated, in the face of the intrusion.

'Gina,' Dai turned to her, an expression almost of entreaty in his eyes, 'this is Linda Green, a near neighbour of mine. She has a key in case my plants need watering while I'm away—or she needs to make free with my supplies. She's always running short of milk and bread,' he explained lamely.

'I'm not nearly as efficient as Dai,' the other woman purred. 'My larder is never as well-stocked as his.' She giggled. 'I'm a disgrace to my sex.'

Dai was clearly supposed to contradict this statement, but he merely directed his level gaze at her. 'Linda, this is a friend and colleague, Gina Barton. We've had a small dinner party and Gina's the last to leave.'

Gina cringed: why should he think it necessary to explain her presence? 'I think I saw you at Jackie and James's party a few weeks ago,' she observed coolly. To her relief, her voice emerged at its usual pitch—neither squeaky nor husky.

'Really? I don't think I had the pleasure of seeing *you*, Miss Barton? Are they friends of yours, then?'

'We were not introduced—I just saw you in the distance. Yes, I know them very well; we live in the same street.'

'*Mrs* Barton,' Dai was busily correcting—evidently

relishing Linda's reaction. 'Or perhaps,' he added, his glance falling to Gina's bare ring-finger, 'you've dropped the title along with the insignia?'

So—he had noticed, although he had refrained from remarking on it before. 'I . . .' she began.

'Gina has a son the same age as Joe,' he interrupted, apparently bent on regaling Linda with her life-history.

The pale plucked brows lifted; the blue eyes widened. 'Is that right? Well well. I work with James, you know—in advertising,' she informed Gina graciously. 'And you work with Dai, do you?' The blue eyes were piercing, burrowing.

'Not exactly. I'm a solicitor. Our firm briefs him from time to time . . .'

'And from time to time,' Dai cut in drily, 'it doesn't.' He shot her a glance; even now, with so many major successes to his credit, her refusal to offer him that one case still rankled.

'I see.' There was something coldly calculating about the way Linda summed up the scene she had just stumbled across. 'Well, I'm sorry to barge in. I wasn't going to use my key, Dai, but when you didn't answer I thought . . . well, something might have happened to you . . .'

Like hell you did, thought Gina.

'As you see,' replied Dai stiffly, 'I was in no danger whatsoever.'

I'm glad someone wasn't, at least, taunted Gina's mind mercilessly.

'As I see.' Linda's brows rose again in wry acknowledgement. 'I'll be off now, then, before I spoil the party.' With an icy smile, in which genuine regret played no part at all, she turned away.

'It seems,' Dai observed, 'that you already have. Goodbye, Linda.'

At the door, she half-turned to flutter her eyelashes at him, all innocence. 'Would you like your key back now, Dai?' she offered.

'That's not necessary.' He followed her to the door. 'But perhaps you'll consider using it only when you know—for a fact—I'm alone; preferably by arrangement.'

The empty smile directed itself at Gina. 'So nice to have met you, Mrs Barton.'

'Good night,' said Gina.

Dai disappeared into the hall with Linda, and Gina heard his brusque tones as he saw her off. When he came back, she was busily tidying her hair. 'I must go,' she announced as soon as he came in.

'Gina—please don't go—I can't tell you how sorry I am this happened . . .'

'I'm not.' Gina's tone was dull; her eyes avoided his pleading gaze.

'Don't say that. She's an idiotic bitch!' he exploded. 'I told her only to use that key when I'd . . . I like someone else to have one,' he explained, almost desperately, 'in case I lock myself out of the flat. I've been known to do that.'

'We've all been known to do that.' Still the curious flatness about her voice—echoing her squashed feelings. 'Good idea for a neighbour to have a key. Saves all sorts of hassles.'

'I knew you'd understand.' He took a step towards her.

'Oh, I understand.' She raised her eyes to meet his. 'I understand.'

'Gina, there's nothing . . . she's just—I'm not . . .' For one, rare second this confident, articulate man groped for words. That sight was something, Gina supposed, to be gleaned from the events of the last ten minutes. 'Please don't . . .'

Suddenly she felt acutely weary. 'Dai, I'm sure there isn't . . . and she isn't. And I won't. All right?' Then, with a sudden burst of spirit, she demanded, 'Anyway—what's it got to do with me? Your . . . neighbourly arrangements are no concern of mine. You're your own man; you've made that clear enough. I'm glad you find some use for members of my feeble sex, since you don't give us credit for much else of any importance. I suppose I should be honoured to be one of the chosen.' She was shocked at her own bitterness, but there was no point in hiding it.

He pulled himself together; some of the familiar arrogance returned to his eyes, to his voice. 'Like I said to Sam, Gina—I'm no monk. There's a lot about me you don't know.'

'That's for sure,' she agreed sardonically. 'But I'm learning fast.'

'Whatever you go away and think,' he implored—and there was the light of sincerity in his face, the ring of it in his tone—'please don't think what was happening to us tonight wasn't real to me. It was.' He moved a step nearer. 'Please?'

She surveyed him for a few moments in silence. 'I'm not sure what I think—yet.' With calm dignity she picked up her bag, and walked steadily up to him. He stood still; waiting, watching. Reaching him, she stood on tiptoe, placing one hand on each of his shoulders to kiss him lightly on the cheek. 'Thank you for a delicious dinner, Dai.'

Without a backward glance she left the room and crossed the hall, grabbing her coat on the way. Then she let herself out through the front door and ran down three flights of stairs—out into the refreshing chill of the night air.

And there at the kerb, her little Metro waited for her—and it was like a staid old friend: a small piece of the security of home.

CHAPTER NINE

TOBY's half-term fell at the beginning of November. On the Monday, Gina took him into the office with her—a treat he greatly approved of but which she kept strictly rationed. He spent most of the day sitting quietly in a corner of the large outer room, behind a small table on which he had piled an impressive array of books: books to read, books to colour, books to draw in, books of games and books of puzzles. He was an industrious, self-sufficient child.

During intervals between these intellectual pastimes he exerted his infallible charm over the clients who passed through the office, as well as on Michele. 'He's gorgeous,' she told Gina as they packed up to go home. 'You can bring him in every day, if you like. Can't she, Toby?'

'I wouldn't dream of it,' Gina asserted. 'Doesn't he get in your way?'

'Not in the least—he's as good as gold,' insisted Michele—who wouldn't have been too upset if he had. She gave him a big hug and kiss as they left, and Toby stood still to suffer them politely.

'Can I come again tomorrow?' he pestered from the back seat as Gina drove them home. 'It's good at your office. I'd like to go there every day. It's much better than school.'

'You wouldn't if you had to,' she assured him sternly. 'You'd soon get bored—and so would Michele. Are you sure you don't bother her when she's working? She has a lot to do, and if I thought you . . .'

'Of course I don't.' He expelled a long-suffering sigh; really, his mother had an unnecessarily suspicious nature. When he said he had things to get on with, she

149

ought to have known that he meant it. 'But she did show me her special typewriter and let me make a few words on it. It's brilliant, Mum. In the middle there's a sort of ball thing, and it moves, and you can put different ones in and make big or small letters. Michele says you can even get one for writing Chinese. *Can* I go again tomorrow?' he persisted hopefully.

'Not tomorrow,' she said. 'You're going to Joe's, remember? Maybe one day later this week, though. We'll see.'

Toby didn't think much of his mother's 'we'll sees'; but he knew there was no point in arguing after he'd heard one. Anyway, it was brilliant at Joe's as well.

At five-thirty on Tuesday evening, Gina was established in Jackie's kitchen behind a steaming mug of tea. 'Sometimes,' she remarked, watching as her friend chopped up an onion on a wooden board, 'I feel like a permanent fixture at this table. Can I do anything to help, Jackie? What are your lucky lot getting tonight?'

'Oh, nothing very spectacular.' Jackie flicked the auburn fringe out of her eyes, smiling round at Gina. 'Just a chicken casserole.'

'Just? Well, I hope they appreciate it.'

'I'm quite certain they do,' Jackie said, with quiet assurance. 'And I appreciate them, Gina—don't forget that. I enjoy all this.'

'I know.' Gina suppressed a tiny, niggling pinpoint of envy.

'As for you doing anything to help,' Jackie took the pieces of onion over to the stove and added them to a pan of sizzling butter. 'I'm fine, but I feel like a chat— so just sit there and talk to me, and you'll be helping. You've been hard at it all day,' she pointed out, with a glance at Gina's rather strained face. 'We've had quite a lazy sort of time here.'

Gina sipped her tea. 'Okay, boss. What shall I talk about?'

'Well, I haven't really seen you for ages. Tell me how everything's been going? How's Brian, for instance? Sam was here the other night, and he was saying . . .'

Gina's head jerked up. 'What?'

'Oh, just that Brian seems a bit—subdued at the moment. Not ill or anything, he thinks; but not his usual cheery self. Has something happened between you, Gina?' She embarked on peeling a panful of potatoes.

'No. Yes.' Why shouldn't she confide in Jackie? She had no one else to talk to; and sometimes she felt she'd burst, keeping it all under such tight control. 'He asked me to marry him, Jackie.'

The auburn eyebrows shot up; she paused with the peeler in one hand and a potato in the other. 'No! Really? What did you say?' The green eyes were alight with intrigue and concern.

'I said no, of course.' It was a bald statement, made in a flat, dull tone.

Jackie's gaze dropped, and she went on peeling for a moment before she replied. 'I suppose you would. What a shame. Poor Brian. He's very keen on you, you know.'

'I do know—now. I wasn't aware just how keen until then. He took me completely by surprise. He was like another person—I was quite frightened.'

'You mean—making demands he hasn't made before; that sort of thing?' Jackie, with her avid curiosity about human nature, was nothing if not shrewd.

'That's exactly what I mean.'

'Poor Brian,' said Jackie again, as if to herself.

'Don't keep saying "poor Brian" like that,' snapped Gina, irritated. 'I feel bad enough about him already. I know I haven't been very fair to him over the last couple of years—but I had to get on with my life, Jackie, and I needed all the support I could get. Can I help it,' she demanded defensively, 'if I don't feel the same way about him as he does about me?'

'Of course not, love.' Jackie put the potatoes into a pan of clean water and left them to boil. Then she came over to sit opposite Gina, nursing her own mug of tea. 'Of course you can't. You never have, and you probably never could. It wouldn't have been honest to accept him. But what brought all this on just now?' Her glance fell to Gina's left hand where it lay on the table. 'I notice you've given up wearing your wedding ring, too, and I did wonder if . . .'

'If what?' interrupted Gina sharply.

'If it had anything to do with Brian. But obviously it hasn't.'

'Not directly,' Gina said carefully. This was the edge of deep and dangerous water, and she felt uneasy about wading into it. 'I am . . . getting a divorce,' she admitted. 'In fact the decree *nisi* is all but through. I decided it was time I stopped hiding behind a nonexistent façade of being married.'

'But not because of Brian?' Jackie pressed. 'Then why?' When Gina failed to reply to this, she leaned closer to ask quietly, 'It wouldn't have anything to do with your friend and mine, Mr Dai Rees, would it?'

Gina looked down into her cup. She might have known Jackie's unerring instinct would home in accurately. But then, in the last analysis, just what *did* her decision have to do with Dai? Nothing, she had frequently told herself, over these last weeks; absolutely nothing. 'It wasn't directly to do with either Brian or Dai,' she said at last, choosing her words with care. 'But indirectly, I think it has connections with both. I can't really explain any more than that.'

'You don't have to explain at all. It's your life. But I'm sure it's a good, positive step to take. I'm with you all the way, Gina—you know that, don't you?'

Gina smiled gratefully. 'I do know. Thanks, Jackie.'

'When I saw you together at our party, and asked James who Dai was,' Jackie remembered with a grin, 'you could have knocked me down with a vol-au-vent. I had no idea he'd be there—and just after we'd been talking about him, too—you remember? When you'd just met him and were sounding off about his conceited prejudices and chauvinist tendencies.'

Gina winced: how could she forget? 'They don't improve, on closer acquaintance.'

'How much closer has your acquaintance got, then?' enquired Jackie blandly.

Gina flicked a glance at her. Her expression appeared artless enough, but you never knew with Jackie—she could be surprisingly devious. 'Professionally, we've had a few more dealings. I didn't brief him on that shoplifting case after all—but you knew that, of course,' she recalled grimly, 'because I came running to you after I'd lost it—cried on your shoulder, as usual.'

'Oh, I know all about professionally,' Jackie announced airily. 'Sam told us plenty about the way the man's career seems to be taking off like a rocket. All these notorious cases he's been involved in—drugs, and libel, and now rape ... I thought he looked dynamic,' she added thoughtfully, 'and obviously he is.'

'You could call him that.' Gina sighed. Dynamism! Was that the quality which had penetrated to every level of her being; taken hold of her memory so that their recent close encounter was continually there with her—however hard she tried to forget it? Lying awake at night, she would attempt yet again to summon up outraged indignation; and all she could manage was a piercing, shooting stab of excitement. Abandoning her feelings to fend for themselves, she found them returning traitorously to the wrong recollections: his confident tenderness; his lively humour; that genuine attention to her needs ...

'But have you seen much of him,' Jackie was probing, 'in an—unprofessional capacity?'

Gina avoided her friend's direct gaze. 'We've been out together a few times, actually,' she admitted. 'We had a meal at a great place—a Bistro, not all that far from here—I wonder if you know it—if not, you should try it . . .'

'Gina.' Smiling, Jackie cut into the flow of desperate diversionary chatter. 'You don't have to tell me anything at all. But before you go on, I ought to be straight with you about one thing: this interrogation isn't just based on educated guesswork. I have . . .' she frowned as she summoned up the legal jargon, 'concrete evidence. Incontrovertible proof, isn't that the expression? Anyway, a first-hand eye witness to the . . . I won't say crime. The event.'

All at once Gina felt exhausted. It seemed the world was ganging up on her, even her best friend and ally. At the same time, realisation dawned: she had been stupid not to think of it before. Linda Green, of course. Linda was a close colleague of James, and would indubitably have rushed to him with such a juicy piece of gossip . . . especially as a means of getting back at Gina, she thought wryly.

Being discovered in Dai's flat—in a state of some . . . disarray—at a late hour of the evening. She closed her eyes. What point was there in trying to maintain some vestige of privacy in the face of such a concerted invasion? 'You are referring,' she said slowly, 'to the fact that Ms Linda Green dropped by on her neighbour and . . . friend, Dai Rees, on a certain evening recently, and happened to find me there, on my own, partaking of a cup of coffee with him?'

'I am referring to that incident.' Jackie leaned across the table, eager in her intent not to hurt her friend—who was quite clearly suffering from a painful mixture of emotions just now. In Jackie's book people needed to air such problems to a sympathetic ear—to get them into perspective. In her opinion, Gina didn't do that nearly enough. 'I take everything our Linda says—and does—with a handful of salt,' she told Gina firmly. 'She's harmless enough really, and very clever at her job; but she's totally unscrupulous, especially when it comes to men. If James wasn't immune to her blandishments, she'd have had hooks into him years ago.'

'Really?' This piece of news shook Gina out of her own defensiveness. 'Jackie—how awful! The cow! How could she?'

Jackie shrugged. 'It was a long time ago; and I trust James. Anyway, he told me all about it at the time. Fortunately he just found it rather funny and a bit pathetic—though his male vanity wasn't above being polished up a bit,' she remembered, with a fond half-smile. 'They're all little boys under the skin, you know. They all crave attention and admiration. Your Dai is just a bit more—overt about it than some, that's all.'

'He's hardly "my Dai",' corrected Gina stiffly.

'Anyway,' Jackie went on, 'as I say, I don't take much notice of Linda usually; she can be very spiteful, and sometimes invents things. But she did seem to be extremely cocky about this little snippet. Then, when Sam said you were all there the other evening, and what a good dinner you had . . .'

'We did. Dai's an excellent cook—among his other accomplishments. And it's a very opulent flat; he has some very fine things. After Sam and Martha had gone—they had to leave quite early,' she explained laboriously, 'I was about to leave too, but he persuaded me to stay for coffee. I suppose one thing led to another, and Linda barged in before . . . just as . . .' She tightened her fingers around her tea mug, knowing her colour was rising. It wasn't easy for her, saying all this—not even to Jackie.

'Before another thing could lead to yet another?' hazarded Jackie with quiet tact.

'That's about it. Actually she did me a good turn, though I'm sure she doesn't think so. He took me by surprise, Jackie. He's very . . . I find him . . .'

'Attractive? I should think you would; so do I!' Jackie declared, with disarming sincerity. 'What little I've seen of him, he's really got something.'

Gina braced herself. Now that she had opened up, she might as well go the whole hog. 'The thing is, I like him too—as a person. If only it wasn't for that one thing—his arrogance, his prejudice against women as . . . functional human beings. He's excellent company, when we're not falling out about that. It gets in the way of everything.'

'Everything?' echoed Jackie meaningfully.

Gina flushed; but she nodded defiantly. 'Everything. That, most of all. He uses women, Jackie—we're hardly more than sex objects to him, I can tell. It's almost as if he despises us, in a way. It was glaringly obvious what his relationship is with Linda. If I let myself, I'd just be another . . . notch in his cane.' She grimaced. 'A piece in his collection. I shall never let that happen to me, Jackie. Never.'

Jackie sat back in her chair, regarding her friend pensively. 'What makes you so sure she's one of a crowd?' she asked gently. 'I don't doubt you're right about her—she'd be only too happy to get her claws as deep into him as possible. The using would be mutual, in her case,' she observed wryly. 'A man like Dai would hardly be likely to turn down an offer like that, right on his doorstep. After all, he's single, isn't he?'

'Singularly single,' Gina conceded.

'Well then—why should you think there are others?' Jackie persisted. 'He might really feel something for you—had you thought of that?'

'Even if there aren't others at this moment,' Gina declared, 'there have been plenty—I'm sure of that. And even if Linda's the only one now—she's one too many for me. As for having feelings . . .' she frowned. 'He may want me, but the only person Dai Rees is ever likely to be in love with is himself. If you ask me, he's incapable of loving any woman—not with that . . . overdeveloped aggression. It's too much of an obstacle.'

'Without it,' Jackie suggested—now well under way with her analysis—'you might accept him, just as he is? You might accept your feelings for him?'

'Without it,' Gina felt a kind of relief, as she admitted the truth to Jackie—and thus to herself—for the first time, 'I'd be in imminent danger of falling in love with the wretched man.'

There was a short pause, while Jackie continued to look thoughtfully at Gina—barely concealing a new expression of amused, affectionate delight; and Gina stared down into the bottom of her teacup, hearing her own words bouncing off the sides of her head with amazed alarm. Had she really said that? Had she meant it?

Eventually, Jackie spoke—softly, kindly. 'I knew there was something about you, Gina. When you took your ring off, and told me about the divorce—and this thing about Brian—and most of all, something about the look and feel of you recently. It all fits together.'

'Don't get too excited,' Gina reminded her grimly. 'There's no future in it. I'm grateful to Dai for bringing matters to a head between me and Brian, and for forcing me to take certain decisions about my life. He's a catalyst, that's all. I understand myself better, thanks to him. And the lovely Linda. When you see her again,' she added defiantly, 'you can tell her from me—she did me a good turn.'

'I don't suppose Dai would agree with you there,' remarked Jackie sagely.

'Do you know,' Gina exploded, enraged at the memory, 'she has her own key to his place?'

'That's probably for entirely practical reasons,' Jackie rationalised. 'Like neighbours often do—letting in the gas board . . . feeding cats . . .'

'Dai hasn't got a cat,' snapped Gina unreasonably.

'Linda has. A rather divine long-haired white Persian. Anyway, you know what I mean, Gina.'

'Oh yes, I know. Borrowing sugar. Watering plants. Keeping an eye on his wellbeing. But don't run away with the idea that I'm jealous, Jackie.'

'Perish the thought!' Jackie frowned; but her eyes were dancing.

'It just came to me, when she appeared, that he'd

planned the whole thing. Getting me there by myself, I mean. He lulled me into a sense of false security, and then—well, if it hadn't been for Linda, he'd have taken full advantage.'

'With no co-operation from you at all?' teased Jackie, now grinning openly.

'Just think how I'd feel now,' Gina insisted, 'if we hadn't been interrupted.' *How would she feel now?* her mind taunted. *Could it be any worse than she felt?*

Jackie's glance was quizzical; but she stood up, looking at her watch. 'Talking of interruptions, I must get on with the supper. James will be home any minute, and those boys have been stuck in front of the goggle-box for hours: their eyes will be square. That reminds me, Gina—it's Joe's birthday on Thursday, you know. We asked him what he'd like to do and he says he wants to go to the Planetarium and then out to tea. Toby's invited, of course. Just drop him round in the morning.'

'How lovely. He's never been to the Planetarium. He'll love that—thanks.'

'The thing is, can he stay the night? Joe likes it when he does, and we're not sure when we'll be back. Then you needn't worry about him—and you'll be free to work late, or even go out for the evening.'

'You are good to me.' Gina sighed. 'I don't know what I'd do without you.'

'Don't sound so miserable about it,' Jackie laughed. 'You know we enjoy having Toby. I keep telling you, Joe's like a different person when he's around. Maybe,' she suggested archly, 'you and Dai might like an evening out?'

'What I'd like,' said Gina, 'is a peaceful, private night in—to unwind, write letters, catch up on some reading, maybe pamper myself a bit, without childish interruptions. That would be my idea of luxury at the moment.'

'Well, whatever you do with it,' Jackie told her, 'Thursday evening's yours.'

*   *   *

Thursday at the office turned out to be one of those days which should have been cancelled early on through lack of support. For a start, it was pouring with rain. Michele had a streaming cold, and sat sneezing behind her desk, croaking pathetically into the telephone and exuding misery and menthol fumes all over the clients. Brian spent the afternoon at Court, where he lost all three cases he was attending. Sam had had a serious row with Martha, and appeared halfway through the morning, looking hangdog and battered. Only Gina was relatively unscathed—on the surface at least—and she fought hard all day to keep everyone going and see that they didn't collapse into total depression.

She arrived home later than usual and utterly worn out. Jackie couldn't have chosen a better night to ask Toby to stay, she reflected as she threw off her damp coat. She only hoped they'd had a good time, and the rain hadn't spoilt the birthday treat. Most of it was indoors, and James would be providing transport in the huge family estate car, so everything had probably gone off fine. Anyway it wasn't her worry—as long as Toby was all right.

After a pot of tea and a plate of scrambled eggs in front of the television, she felt greatly restored and settled down to write some long-overdue letters. At nine she repaired to the bathroom with a paperback novel, and soaked herself—and it—in a deep, hot, scented bath for forty minutes. This was a luxury she rarely allowed herself, and it was her idea of heaven—even if the pages did end up a bit like papier maché by the time she forced herself to get out. They usually dried off again quite satisfactorily—if a little curly at the edges.

She was just giving her dripping hair a vigorous towelling when the doorbell rang. Doorbells! She sighed: perhaps she should have disconnected hers tonight—the one night she had promised herself unbroken peace and seclusion. It was late for visitors, anyway. Perhaps it was Brian again, come to make amends ... she didn't really miss her outings with him, but it was a bit uncomfortable at the office. Or perhaps it was James or Jackie, come to collect something for Toby—had she forgotten to pack his toothbrush? His pyjamas? No, she remembered putting them both into his little bag. Her heart thumped slightly: could anything be wrong, down the road? Perhaps Toby had had an accident?

The bell was still ringing impatiently. Pulling on her cream velour dressing gown, and winding a towel round her head, turban fashion, she ran down the short flight of stairs to the hall and opened the front door an inch or two, putting on the chain first. 'Who is it?' She peered out into the murky night.

'It's me.' The figure looming on the doorstep was large and powerful; his voice deeper, closer than she had expected, startling her. 'Hallo, Gina.'

'Dai! What the hell are you doing here?'

'Well now, that's a fine welcome for a chap on a filthy night. Here I come, seeking comfort and succour, and the lady swears at me!' the deep voice lamented.

'Why do you need comfort and succour?' she demanded suspiciously. 'And why have you come looking for it here?'

'If you let me in,' he pointed out reasonably, 'I can tell you.'

'But I'm not ... decent,' she protested. 'And I'm having ...'

'That's quite all right. I like my women indecent: you know that.' He turned up his coat collar and shivered ostentatiously. 'Come on, Gina—let me in. Just for a few minutes. I won't eat you; and it's chucking it down out here.'

There was no harm, she supposed, in allowing him in as far as the hall, if he had something specific to say. Curiosity got the better of caution, and she took the chain off. Immediately, unceremoniously, he pushed the door open and walked straight past her into the hall. 'That's better. Keeping a poor man on the doorstep on a night like this. Where are your manners, woman?' He took off his wet coat and hung it on a hook.

She slammed the door shut behind him, clutching her dressing gown together with one hand and holding on to her turban, which had come seriously adrift, with the other. 'As it happens, it's not very convenient this evening. I'm rather busy.'

The acute grey gaze travelled the length of her unprotected form. 'What do you mean? You don't look very busy. Aren't you alone?' His eyes flashed cynicism. 'Surely you're not too busy to spare a man a cup of coffee?'

She made a helpless gesture with her hands. 'I was trying,' she told him, in a resigned tone, 'to snatch a few quiet hours to myself.'

'Surely Toby hasn't been in bed all that long? It's half-term, isn't it?'

'Toby's away.' The moment she'd said it, she could have bitten her tongue out. Fool that she was—not to keep from Dai, of all people, the fact that Toby wasn't there. Toby—whose presence was her best protection, her bodyguard. But it was done now; she lifted her chin defiantly. 'He's only down the road at Jackie's.'

'Near enough to be summoned at a moment of crisis?' he sneered. 'But far enough to permit you a nice little uninterrupted evening? How convenient!' He leaned against the wall, eyes narrowed on her face. For the first time she noticed the strange, harsh gleam in them; the new, determined twist to the mouth. It was almost as if he was drunk—and yet she could swear it wasn't anything like that.

Involuntarily she backed away, one foot on the bottom stair—poised for escape. 'If you're staying, I must go and get some clothes on. Then I'll make us some coffee,' she promised breathlessly. Anything to evade that level, piercing stare.

He took a step towards her. 'No need to run away from me, Gina. I keep telling you—I won't hurt you. I won't do anything you don't want me to do.'

'Why are you here now, Dai? Tonight? You've never come round like this before.'

'Maybe I thought it was about time I did,' he declared smoothly. 'And since you didn't invite me, I took matters into my own hands. Seems I chose an auspicious evening.' His voice vibrated with undercurrents she could hardly miss. Still facing him defensively, she stepped up on to the lowest stair; and he moved another pace closer so that her gold-brown eyes were directly on a level with his stone-grey ones. It was a new angle on him—more hypnotic than ever.

'To be truthful, Gina, I didn't just come by chance tonight,' he was saying—still in that same low, urgent tone. 'And I misled you—I'm not really after succour and support. Quite the reverse, in fact. I've had a major success today, and I want to share it with you. I wanted you to be the first to know.'

'Why me?' she breathed, mesmerised by the power in his eyes. What was left of her sensible mind fought to understand the difference in him—what was it? More than the usual arrogance, there was a twist of cruelty there somewhere—of brutality, even. 'Why not?' he countered softly.

She shivered inwardly; but she spoke firmly. 'I'm glad you've had a success, Dai. But surely that's routine for you by now, isn't it?' A note of sarcasm hardened her voice. 'I mean, if you'd *lost* a case, that might be something to get worked up about—but winning—well, that's no more than we've all come to expect of the great Advocate Rees, isn't it?'

The towel had slipped off completely now, and lay on the floor at her bare feet, leaving her hair to tumble over her shoulders and back—damp but still richly dark and shining. His eyes caressed it, briefly, and then returned to drill into hers. 'Ah, but this one, my dear Gina,' he grated, 'is just a little bit special. This one was a tough nut to crack—but it appears, from today's hearing, that I have cracked it.'

She folded her arms, leaning against the banister—collecting as much poise as she could muster. 'You're obviously dying to tell me, so you might as well get it over with.'

Her defiance pushed him over the edge. His hands reached out to cup her face, clamping her head while his gaze became more intense than ever. 'Wouldn't you rather show me round your flat first? Isn't it about time you returned my hospitality?' he growled dangerously. 'I've been waiting for the invitation.'

She fought to escape from the iron grip; but she could scarcely speak, let alone move her head, with those fingers tight on her jaw. 'You can go on waiting!' she spat, teeth and fists clenched in anger and alarm. Then, with an inner struggle, she managed to regain her control for a moment. 'If you let me go upstairs and get some clothes on,' she pointed out, 'I might consider it.'

'What's all this obsession with clothes?' he mocked. His face was moving—infinitely slowly, it seemed—nearer to hers. 'Who needs clothes? You're far more desirable without them—as I should know,' he reminded her softly, suggestively. When his mouth was only inches from hers, and she could feel the warmth of his breath on her skin, smell the spicy male tang of him, he whispered, 'I'd like to see your bedroom, Gina. Show me; now.'

Then his lips were hard on hers, and this time their invasion was instant and total. All that subtle restraint—that seductive tenderness—had exploded into a strident, insistent demand which left her reeling, gasping—face bruised, mouth swollen under the grinding pressure of his assault.

She pushed and twisted to free herself; but even as she did it, the first embers of latent desire were igniting themselves deep within her—becoming leaping flames, and then a roaring, pulsating wildfire which took hold and spread through every fibre of her weak frame. He was without mercy, and she was without shame; and there, at the foot of Gina's staircase on a wet Thursday night, the two of them locked into a battle as ancient, as violent, as endless as the human race itself.

His hands abandoned her burning cheeks to force their way into the soft folds of her robe—which lay, within seconds, discarded on the ground next to her towel. With this last layer of protection gone, she gave up all pretence of struggle. Her body accepted—welcomed—the inevitable. Her mind howled out one faint, final protest before vanishing into a red limbo of passion.

Gina barely remembered it later—the process of climbing the few stairs, of reaching her bedroom—welded together all the way, pausing at every step to deepen their explorations of each other. She was dimly aware that they fell, as one unit, on to the neat double bed in the tidy, pretty room; and that the next moment Dai's muscular body was naked beside her own softly rounded one. She knew that her hands were running themselves over it, discovering its lines and shapes and angles and textures—the smoothness of his skin, the wiriness of his hair—without any bidding from her. She knew that his fingers and mouth were equally busy—expertly moulding, seeking, urging her flesh to a peak of yearning delight.

Then there was the whirlwind: the piling of tension upon tension, sensation upon sensation—and the strange, far-off echoes of her own cries, like memories of a haunting, long-forgotten song; and his groans—alien sounds, and yet somehow part of her. After that, the explosion—a release, a revelation her body had craved and been denied for far, far too many long months . . . and then the silence. That profound, absolute silence which only exists between two separate people when they have ceased, for a short while, to be separate.

And then, into the silence, crept the reaction. First those niggling, irritating little doubts—fed through from her ever-active mind, still ticking over even now; rapidly expanding into self-despising regrets, which twisted themselves round against him so that all the negative feelings went his way, and it was all his fault, and she hated him with all her heart; and tears rolled down her cheeks and on to his arm, which pillowed her head.

He shifted his weight from on top of her. 'Gina?' The voice was hoarse; the word itself seemed unfamiliar. 'Are you all right?' He propped himself on one elbow to look down into her face.

'No. I'm not.'

Concern flooded into his features, pushing out the residue of passion. 'What's wrong? I didn't hurt you, did I?'

'Not physically.'

'I didn't think I had,' he murmured complacently, bending to nuzzle her earlobe. 'Nothing to cry about, Gina. It was inevitable; you know that, as well as I do.'

She heaved against him with all her strength and rolled out from under him, to stand trembling beside the bed. Her face was contorted in a glare of rage. 'How can you be so—so smug, Dai—after all your protestations about nothing happening unless we both wanted it to . . . so much for your promises . . .' she could hardly speak in her blind fury.

'Gina Barton.' He sat up, running a hand through his hair. 'Don't come the wronged maiden with me. You wanted it as much as I did. You wanted *me*,' he corrected carefully, 'as much as I wanted *you*. Why bother to go through all this performance of pretending you didn't? It's such a waste of time and effort, that part of it.' He sighed, world-weary. 'Women never seem to be able to take what they want without all this fuss afterwards.'

'Oh, they never do, do they?' she snarled. 'Could

that be because you feel free to take what *you* want, just exactly when you want it, how and where and as you want it—whatever they might really need?'

'If we waited for women to know what they "really need",' he returned, with exaggerated patience, 'the human race would have died out centuries ago. Fortunately we know better than they do.'

'Of all the obnoxious, opinionated, overblown ...' Words failed her, and she could only stare at him, fists clenched, eyes flashing. Then she became acutely conscious of her nakedness, her vulnerability (*too late! too late!* her mind harped), and grabbed the jeans and sweatshirt which happened to be hanging on the chair by her bed. 'You're an immoral opportunist, Dai Rees. You'd have taken advantage of me before, if your little plan had worked out—now you've achieved your end by sheer surprise. You're disgusting—the lowest of the low.' She climbed into her clothes, still glaring.

He failed to rise to her anger—which only served to increase it. 'I didn't notice you turning tail and running on either occasion, Gina,' he observed mildly. 'Are you really so incapable of voicing a negative if you want to? And even if your mind wanted to,' he pointed out, with infuriating accuracy, 'your body was sending me very different messages. Do you really regret listening to them?' he asked, with quiet persistence.

The fact that his confidence was well-founded did nothing to improve her temper. 'You'd better go, Dai.' Safely covered, she felt less desperate. 'Get your clothes on and leave. And don't come back.' Turning, she left him alone in the bedroom and stormed downstairs.

Five minutes later he was in the hall, fully dressed, totally poised. 'Do you really want me to go, Gina?' Contrition was the last thing on his mind as his eyes sparked, locking with hers, forcing her body to recall those recent minutes it had shared with his. His hand came out to stroke her cheek. 'Really?'

She flinched from the touch—or rather, from her response to it; then she moved away from him to open the front door. 'Really.' She waited, hand on the handle.

'Wouldn't you even like to know why I came to see you tonight? What my moment of glory was all about today?' he taunted, hands in pockets, eyes gleaming.

'Your *other* moment of glory, you mean,' she said coldly. 'I dare say you're going to tell me, whether I want to know or not. Just get it over with,' she flared, wishing he'd disappear—out of her home, out of her life.

'I will tell you, because you'll find it—relevant.' Again she detected that odd expression of cold triumph which had been in his face when he arrived. 'It was the rape case—you know—the one Sam was talking about the other night? A real humdinger of a challenge. No one thought I'd get the bloke off—royal connections or not. He had everything against him: public opinion, that little girl, hardly a legal leg to stand on—but we did it!' His eyes flashed; his grin was almost manic. 'I did it,' he amended, 'today.'

An icy coldness spread through her, permeating her eyes, her voice. 'I'm so happy for you, Dai. That "little girl" will probably never be the same again, after her experience—but I'm sure she was glad to sacrifice such a small thing in order to further your burgeoning career.'

His eyes darkened. 'Don't be a fool, Gina. You know nothing about it. As it happens, he *was* telling the truth—her family made it all up—they had their reasons—I can't go into it all now.'

'How convenient for you to believe all that,' she retorted. 'I suppose it makes it a bit easier to salve your conscience if you do—but I'm not sure which of us is the fool, Dai. Well, now that he's had his way with her and got away with it; and you've had your way with me and got away with it, perhaps you'll go away and leave me alone, once and for all.'

'Gina, you're being ridiculous. Let me tell you more about it—please.' For a few moments, at least, he had the grace to look a little anxious.

But she had had enough. 'I can see it made a perfect symmetry for you, Dai—coming here tonight—adding me to your list of achievements. It's a pity you and your grateful client didn't remember that it takes two to create that particular scenario—a victim as well as a victor.' Pointedly, she opened the door.

'You're no victim, Gina,' he growled. 'You're a little idiot. You got just as much out of it as I did, if you'd only admit it to yourself. What's the point of rejecting the good things life has to offer you?'

'I don't wish to hear any more.' She gestured to the great outdoors, where it was still raining heavily. 'Please go.'

'Okay, Mrs Barton, okay. I'm going. I've gone.' He shrugged into his coat and stood on the threshold. 'Pity,' he mused—his glance now resting on her thoughtfully, mockingly. 'I was hoping I might persuade you, after my success today, to change your mind about that little case of yours. I told myself that you could hardly refuse to let me take it now, after such results. But I expect I was wrong about that too.'

'You have never,' she assured him icily, 'been more wrong about anything in your life. If I ever had even the slightest intention of changing my mind, I wouldn't now.'

'I always said women were irrational. Now I know it for certain.' He turned and ran down the steps. On the pavement, he swung round to look up at her again. The lamplight reached eerily through the wall of rain to touch his angular features; the glistening droplets on his hair. 'Goodbye, Gina.'

Her only reply was to close the door firmly behind him. Alone inside, she leaned back against it—fighting a terrible blackness which swamped her very soul.

CHAPTER TEN

AFTER that Gina's life became a kind of Purgatory—an endless, featureless tunnel. Even the ostrich technique failed dismally: the more frantically she burrowed, the more it was obvious that escape would never be found in that direction. Deep down in the dark sand there was nothing but her own feelings—and in that department, everything was utter confusion.

She had been let off lightly, her mind constantly lectured, discovering the true nature of the man before further damage could be inflicted. One unfortunate episode—when he had, in effect, bulldozed his way into her home, into her arms—could be overlooked, discounted. Any more, and the responsibility would have to be shared equally—and then who knew what admissions, what openings-up, might follow? No—a strict regime of work and furious activity, that was the prescription; time and application would heal any little residual wounds.

But what about us? cried her body and her heart, every night—as the hours stretched out, longer and lonelier, and the days shortened to the trough of the year. Why did they suffer this sensation of loss—of bereavement, almost—which wouldn't go away? Why this tortured craving for the sight of that one face, the sound of that voice, the touch of those hands—when all they had yet caused her was regret and disruption?

Somewhere far inside herself, in the place where truth refuses to be squeezed out, Gina knew the answer. Disruption was only one word for what Dai Rees had brought her. He had also, through the sheer power of his will, dragged her anaesthetised emotions out of their stupor; bullied them into emerging, weakened and quivering, into the glare of reality. He had slaked the very edge of a profound thirst, satisfied only the barest pangs of a gnawing hunger. And now she was left to soothe her re-awakened self as best she could. As the cold, empty weeks crept by, the message became starkly clear: she couldn't. For once her mind had met its match. The rest of her was winning, all the way.

But Gina's will wasn't lacking in power, either. She wasn't giving in that easily. She gritted her teeth, folded herself inwards and carried on from day to day. Her usually healthy appetite diminished and she lost weight; her normally serene expression became pinched and tense. Friends and colleagues noticed, of course, but she couldn't—wouldn't—confide in anyone, not even Jackie. It wasn't a cut-and-dried problem, like a death or the end of a marriage; there was nothing, really, to be described or discussed. So she clung to her privacy, hoping against hope that scar tissue would form soon; that the raw suffering would give way to a dull ache and then fade.

If there was the slightest chance that it might, Dai himself ensured it never did. After a few days' silence, just as she reached a plateau of relative peace, his voice would be there in her ear—resonant with intimate confidence, shattering the little she had achieved. When he 'phoned her at home she simply replaced the receiver without a word, but she could hardly refuse to speak to him at the office. Though she kept their professional dealings to an absolute minimum, it would have excited too much unwelcome speculation if she had ruled them out altogether. When Michele announced that he was on the line for her, she had no option but to accept the call—but she made sure her words were curt, her attitude stony.

Even so, he pushed aside her barriers on several occasions, coming straight to the point. 'Am I still in the doghouse, Gina?' he would demand, and she could see the glint in his eyes as clearly as if he stood before her. 'Come out with me just once, and I promise you won't regret it.' Or: 'Hasn't this charade gone on long enough, Mrs Barton? Isn't it time you crawled out of your hole—stopped hiding away like a terrified mouse? You and I both know,' he taunted—his tone low and suggestive—'you're no mouse. You can't run away for ever.'

'Thank you for the advice, Dai,' she would reply tersely, 'but we have nothing more to give each other. It was my mistake, letting it get as far as it did. Now just leave me alone.'

'Strange—that wasn't the impression I got,' he drawled. 'I'd have said we had plenty more to give each other. I'd have said we'd hardly started.'

'I don't want to see you,' she lied grimly. 'I want you to get out of my life.'

'Are you sure?' he mocked. 'Don't you miss me— not even a little?'

She winced. Perhaps if he'd tried more gentle, persuasive tactics—if that arrogant self-assurance had cracked open to reveal just a glimpse of a vulnerable centre . . . but there was no way that could happen, not to Dai Rees. His moment of victory had only reinforced that massive male pride so that he was all the more determined to repeat it. She stiffened against the stirrings of temptation to give way—to try again, just once more. 'Not even a little,' she lied again, resolutely.

'It's your loss,' he pointed out with smooth conceit, 'as much as mine, Gina.'

'I dare say I shall survive.' Cold, heavy sarcasm was her only weapon against the sick wave of pain which shook her.

'Well, you know where I am,' he reminded her breezily, 'if you change your mind.'

'I never shall,' she declared through clenched teeth. *Not while you're the person you are, Dai Rees*: the unspoken words pounded through her tormented brain.

* * *

Suddenly—she was never quite sure how it had stealthily arrived—Christmas was upon them. London was alive with festive celebrations, bright lights, gaudy decorations. There were parties to attend, presents to wrap, mince pies to bake—and if Gina secretly wished she could hibernate right through it all, she owed it to Toby to enter into the spirit of the time as far as possible. Like any other seven-year-old he was beside himself with excited anticipation.

Her parents always expected them for the holiday itself; and she handed over the responsibility of entertaining their grandson with more grateful relief than usual. Taking one look at her when she got out of her car on Christmas Eve, they exchanged frowns of concern. But they concentrated all their attentions on Toby—making sure he was having a warm family Christmas—until he was safely tucked up in bed, propping his drooping eyelids open. (This was the year, he'd decided, when he'd finally catch Santa red-handed. Somehow he never managed to stay awake; but this time he was definitely going to.)

Then, in the peace of the country evening, they allowed loving anxiety to overcome their natural reticence, bracing themselves to ask Gina if she was all right—if there was anything they could do. Smiling wanly at those familiar faces—still handsome, both of them, in middle age—Gina assured her parents that she wasn't ill, but that it was nothing she could explain to them—not yet.

'You know we only ask because we care so much about you, darling.' Her mother, even after many years in England, displayed the emotional honesty of her Latin upbringing.

'I do know, thanks, Mum.' Gina looked down at her hands, clasped tightly in her lap, wishing she could peel back the years and let her parents comfort it all away.

Her father added his support—more matter-of-fact, but affectionately tender. 'Just remember we're here if you need anything at all, Gina. We won't say any more—but if you want to talk to us—well, we're always here.'

'I know that too, Dad.' She raised her eyes to theirs now, and her smile was warm behind the veil of pain. 'I'm grateful to you both. One day I'll tell you all about it—but please don't worry,' she implored them. 'I'd hate you to do that. Let's give Toby a good time, and try and have one ourselves too.'

And, rather to her own surprise, they did.

The world shook off its Christmas sluggishness as the new year got under way. Gina realised with a curious jolt that Dai hadn't been in touch at all for days. Not that she'd have expected him to over the holiday— he'd probably spent it with his family in Wales—but there had been plenty of time since. Somewhere, mingled with her relief, she was aware of a new desolation.

It was high time, she also realised, that she was contacting John Slade about the Haines case, which was due to come up for its Appeal in a fortnight. As soon as offices were back to civilised hours, she telephoned his Chambers.

'I'm sorry, Mrs Barton,' the clerk informed her wearily. 'Mr Slade is still in America.'

'But I thought he was due back last month?' Taken aback at the news, Gina snapped more accusingly than she had intended.

'He was; but he decided to stay on over the holiday.' The clerk's tone indicated that Mr Slade's affairs were hardly his responsibility, and he wished people would stop suggesting they were. 'He'll probably be back this week,' he added reluctantly.

'I see. Thank you.' Could she risk leaving it that long? Gina decided she could. As she had reassured Peggy Haines, a barrister needed only a few days in which to prepare a simple defence. After that—well, there were plenty of other good fish in the sea, even if they weren't all as reliable as John. The fact that one of the best of them was Dai Rees, she didn't even acknowledge.

That evening she put Toby to bed early and settled down to some work. As usual, a few days' closure of the office had resulted in a snowstorm of paper on everyone's desks. It was hard to say where it generated from, in the middle of a public holiday, but it always happened—and Gina always ended up bringing some of it home to wade through in peace and quiet.

She was destined for little peace or quiet tonight, it seemed. Half an hour into her concentration, the doorbell issued its peremptory summons. Gina stretched, yawned and sighed. Well, perhaps she'd allow herself a short break—deal with whoever it was, then make herself a quick cup of coffee . . .

Dai's rugged form filled the doorway—imprinting itself on her eyes, fitting itself into the jagged space in her heart which had been torn open for so long. The lost piece of the puzzle; the missing corner of the pattern. It took every ounce of her strength not to hold out her arms to him—but she recovered her composure in time to greet him with a poised, icy stare.

'This is an unexpected . . . surprise.' She took care not to say 'pleasure', not even satirically. In any case it was true: a surprise it certainly was. Even before his persistent 'phone calls had faded off into a bleak silence, one thing he had never even attempted to do, since that tumultuous night, was to appear unannounced on her doorstep.

If she expected a crisp, clever reply she was disappointed. 'Hallo, Gina,' was all he said—and his tone was dull, deadened.

She glanced up sharply now—and stepped back, shocked. There was a change in him which mirrored her own. The fierce, fiery spark had been glassed over; the aggressive confidence trimmed to a shadow of itself. The fine features were still potent enough, but there were lines of strain round eyes and mouth which certainly hadn't been there a few weeks earlier.

He stood motionless—the luminous gaze steady on hers, but without challenge. She returned it for long seconds; and when she spoke, the words were quietly cool. 'What is it, Dai? Why have you come?'

'I've got to speak to you, Gina. Please let me come in. There's something—two things—I must tell you.'

She continued to look at him dubiously. There was sincerity in his voice—deep and vibrant—and it was reflected in his face; but surely she'd be a fool to trust him now? 'I don't know,' she faltered, uncertain.

He held out both hands, pleading; but he made no move towards her. 'Please, Gina,' he repeated vehemently. 'You have my word that I won't—try anything. Just a few minutes, that's all I ask—but I must see you alone. I must talk to you—now, tonight. It's important.'

She deliberated, fast. There was something in the low urgency of his request—and it was a request, not a demand—something which defied her to ignore it. And Toby was asleep upstairs; and not even Dai would take advantage of a situation knowing the child might wake at any moment. Making up her mind, she opened the door fully to him. 'Come in.'

He smiled slightly as he walked past her—making no attempt to touch her. But her flesh tingled as she led him to the sitting room—feeling those eyes upon it all the way—knowing they penetrated through her jeans and sweater to the warm softness beneath, evoking dangerous memories which lurked only just below the surface. He sprawled in an armchair, and she perched on the edge of another, keeping a safe distance between them. Refusing her offer of coffee or a drink, he stretched out long, denim-clad legs and clasped square fingers behind his tangled head, grinning across at her. She suppressed an answering smile—reserved, on her guard. For all she knew, this subdued version of the man might be no more than another of his ploys to get where he wanted to be.

'You said you had something to tell me,' she prompted briskly, when he appeared to be content just to study her with unmasked appreciation.

'Yes, I did. I do.' His gaze became serious. 'It's so good to see you again, Gina. It's been a long time. You look ... thinner—but no less beautiful.' His tone seemed unfamiliar—wistful, almost.

'It's only been a few weeks,' she countered stiffly—taking the upper hand. 'Please say what you came to say, Dai, because I ...'

With a visible effort he shook himself into action, sucking in a long breath. 'Right. Well—you remember when you asked me about the time I was studying for the Bar, and how I financed myself through it?'

'Of course I do.' She tried not to show her surprise. Of all the subjects he might have been going to raise, she hadn't expected this. 'You were diffident about it, to say the least,' she recalled wryly.

'I had my reasons. I rarely tell anyone—I don't like my private life aired in public.'

'So I gathered.' She smiled slightly.

'It was specially important that you shouldn't know this then; but now I want to tell you.' He paused; for a man with such verbal mastery, he was clearly having a struggle to find the words. Gina sat quite still—watching, listening, waiting. 'Just a year through my training, when I was still very young, I got married.' He paused again to let this sink in. 'She was a bit older than me—absolutely brimming over with vitality and creative drive. I thought she was wonderful—she really knocked me out.'

Gina fought back an unreasonable rush of jealousy which attacked her on all fronts. Controlling it, she nodded—her expression placid but her curiosity sharply whetted. 'She was just starting up in business on her own,' he went on—haltingly, as if the recollection was painful. 'A top-class secretarial agency, actually. She was clever, super-efficient, forceful, dominant, sexy, knew all the right people

—or if she didn't, made it her business to meet them . . .'

'Sounds like an amazing lady,' observed Gina; and she meant it.

He pursed up his mouth—rueful, ironic. 'Amazing— oh yes, she was that all right. Got things organised, achieved things, did my wife.' There was resentment stirring there now; harsh bitterness, creeping in round the edges. Gina's quick ear did not miss it, but she instictively held her peace, allowing him to let it out in his own time. 'Before very long she'd built up a regular little empire—was coining money hand over fist—while I . . . I battled on manfully . . .' He laughed without humour—self-deprecatingly—at his own use of the word. 'She earned more than enough to support us both in style, and finance my studies. She went from strength to strength. She loved every minute of it.'

He seemed to have reached a block, so Gina gave him a gentle push. 'And you?'

'I wouldn't have minded, Gina. But she began to . . . flaunt it in front of me; all that success. It gave her such power, and she never hesitated to use it. The very qualities I'd admired in her so much at first—the ones which had made me want her . . . they turned bad and became like so many knives twisting in a festering wound.' The old rage sparked in his eyes. It seemed to Gina that she was seeing him clearly for the first time. It was like a curtain lifting from a view which had been hazy, obscured. The puzzle was falling into place.

'What happened in the end?' she pressed, now genuinely eager to know.

'Oh, I got through my exams, did my pupillage— then as soon as I could, I started making something of myself. She didn't like that one bit.' The bitterness was near to overflowing, but he mastered it and carried on. 'She soon drifted off after other, even younger examples of the species—vulnerable, clinging males who could satisfy her overdeveloped maternal instinct—if that's what it was. Certainly, real children came nowhere on her list of priorities,' he remembered sadly.

'I doubt whether that was what it was,' Gina commented, half to herself.

'Well, whatever her motives, she had no more time for me. Eventually she walked out altogether, and I can't say I was sorry. Took some other worthy cause under her capable wing—just starting out in medicine, I think he was—and he wasn't the last, I believe. We were divorced within two years; I've never seen her since. But I resolved never—ever—to let a woman walk all over me again. Okay, so one helped me on to the first rung of the ladder—but once I was there, I was staying on top. And they were staying where they belonged . . .' he glared fiercely at her for a second; then slumped, exhausted.

'Underneath?' Gina supplied, without rancour. Anger would have been out of place. She was just one of a string of women who had paid the high price he exacted on behalf of that dominating ex-wife. It was no one's fault; it was just one of those things—as it had been in her own marriage, when she had supported her drifting husband through his own college days . . . 'But surely that didn't have to mean we were all the absent-minded, brainless creatures you make us out to be?' She was studying him now with calm interest. 'After all, if she hadn't been like that . . .'

'It was more convenient for me to decide most of you were,' he admitted gloomily. 'And apart from her, I did seem to encounter more than my share of fluffy, empty-headed women. Maybe I deliberately chose to seek their company . . . I don't know . . .'

'Maybe you did,' agreed Gina, wry amusement twitching a corner of her mouth.

'But not you, Mrs Barton!' The statement was an explosion. 'You were something different again—you didn't seem to fit in with any of my preconceived images—so serene, so unpushy; and yet so strong . . . you exerted some profound, subtle influence over me, Gina, without ever once being anything other than supremely, superbly female. I didn't know what had hit me. I only knew one way to fight back. After I'd taken what I wanted, I thought I'd regain control, but . . .' he lifted his hands and dropped them again, helpless.

She shuddered inwardly at this direct reminder; but her gaze never wavered from his. 'And didn't you, Dai?'

A flood of passion had invaded his face and voice now. 'Control? It's deserted me altogether, Gina! For the last few weeks—for the first time in my life—I've been behaving like a lunatic. I've gone around in a crazy daze. At first I told myself it would pass; but the longer I've gone on not seeing you, the worse it's been. And then, the other day . . .' he buried his face in his hands. 'It came to a head. I really blew everything.'

She stilled the flutterings of delight which his words were awakening in her heart, schooling herself to listen impassively. 'Why? What happened?'

'I crashed my car,' he groaned.

'You did *what*?' There was no greeting this piece of news with equanimity. His Lancia—his pride and joy? Come to think of it, she hadn't noticed it in the road when he arrived—but then she'd hardly been in a fit state to notice anything. 'Were you hurt? Was it bad?'

He nodded despondently. 'A write-off. I went straight into a garage wall. I was incredibly lucky to escape with minor lacerations and bruises. They've healed already—but there are deeper scars which will never leave me, Gina.'

'Dai, I'm so sorry—that lovely car! But thank God you were all right. Tell me how it happened,' she invited, leaning towards him eagerly.

'It happened,' he replied, with slow deliberation, 'through plain, unmitigated stupidity. A marathon dose of male absent-mindedness,' he emphasised sardonically. 'My mind was elsewhere, and I failed to take a bend properly. Fortunately, there was no one else about—it was no one's fault but mine. I sheered into this brick wall. I smashed up my car. I made a fair old mess of the wall. And in among the general destruction,' he told her, with wry honesty, 'my overblown ego took a major bashing into the bargain. Not before time, I dare say you're thinking—and you're quite right, too.'

He looked so comically dejected that Gina had to bite her lip to prevent herself from laughing aloud. 'Oh, Dai ... I really am sorry about your car, but at least you weren't hurt—not physically. As for your battered ego, I expect we can patch it up between us.' One finger on her chin, she studied him intently, mischief in her gold-flecked gaze. 'Whatever was your mind so busy about, such a long way from where it ought to have been?' she speculated—all innocence.

He ran a hand through his hair. 'Do you need to ask, woman? I was thinking about you, of course. I haven't stopped thinking about you for two minutes on end since I first set eyes on you.' Suddenly he was on his feet, striding over to kneel beside her, seizing her hands in his. 'You've won, Gina. On behalf of your fair sex, you've beaten me into submission. I'm a broken man.' He sighed deeply, glancing at her from under downcast lashes.

'Oh, I do hope not, Dai. You wouldn't be much use to me—or any of us—if you were.'

He looked up then, straight into the joyful glow of her eyes. 'Well—perhaps I've retained some of my fighting spirit,' he confessed. 'Enough to take you on for a few more rounds, on equal terms—if you'll accept the challenge?' he invited humbly, his hands tightening their grip on hers. 'I swear I'll never make such ridiculous generalisations about women—or anything else—again.'

'Promises—rash promises,' she whispered fondly,

'but I accept your challenge.' She leaned over to kiss him on the cheek; and then she was enfolded in his arms, and they were holding each other as if their sanity, their very lives, depended on the warm contact.

'Of course,' he muttered into her ear, somewhat later, 'you realise I only came to you for one thing?'

She broke away to peer into his face. 'And what might that be—as if I didn't know?'

'Oh, it's not what you're thinking. I haven't got a car any more, remember? It was towed away ignominiously at the end of a chain. Until I decide what to do next, I'm without transport of my own.' He hung his head. 'And you know how I hate the Tube,' he grumbled.

'Let me get this straight, Dai. *You* are actually asking *me*—a mere female—to drive you around?' Surely this was the ultimate irony. It was all Gina could do to suppress a giggle.

'Not just asking,' he confirmed solemnly. 'Begging. I'm here this evening, Gina, to implore you to be my chauffeuse—at least once in a while.'

'Hmm.' She thought about it. 'That'll take some consideration. It can be dangerous, you know, driving a passenger who's inclined to be a bit ... unpredictable.'

He flinched; then he squared his shoulders. 'I deserve it all. Don't spare me, Gina—whatever you throw at me, I'll take it like a man.' And he proceeded, very soon and very thoroughly, to provide incontrovertible proof of that claim.

A long time later—when she lay across his lap, her rumpled clothes and hair and expression barely recognisable as belonging to the same neat, collected young woman who had answered the door a couple of hours before—he dragged his lips from hers just long enough to score one last point. 'You know,' he murmured, 'after this, there's no way you can refuse to let me take on the Haines case.'

'So that's what all this is about!' she marvelled,

winding her fingers in the vital mane of his hair, forcing his head back so that she could look into his eyes. 'Ulterior motives in all directions—how devious men are!'

'I happen to know,' he persisted, 'that Slade's still away. Have you instructed anyone else instead yet?'

'Actually, no.' Her gold-brown eyes were brightly reflective behind their cloud of passion.

'Well then.' He was keen, hopeful, like a child. 'Gina—my sweet, my cariad—let me do it for you?' he wheedled.

Her smile was a slow, spreading radiance—a sunrise. 'Of course I'll let you; you're right,' she said softly, 'after this, there's no way I could refuse you—not that, or anything else.'

Regent's Park was lively on a crisp Saturday morning in early March. It had snowed, sleeted, frosted and hailed; but already the first daffodils, crocuses and tulips were bravely pushing their green tips out through the cold soil.

Gina, who felt as if it had been the longest winter of her life, sat on a wooden bench, turning her face up to welcome the rays of a clean, new sun. A line of poetry arrived in her head from somewhere, and she repeated it aloud to herself, savouring its sound and its message. *If winter comes, can spring be far behind?*

Then she opened her eyes and looked across to where, twenty yards away, a tall man and a small boy were busy kicking a football around on the grass. Really, there was little to choose between the two of them, apart from the fact that one was about twice the height of the other . . . their old jeans and thick roll-neck sweaters could have been a uniform. The small fair head and the bigger dark one were equally tousled. The concentration they were each putting into their game was equally intense.

She smiled as they ran towards her, Toby carrying the muddy ball under one arm. 'I saved all Dai's goals,' he announced proudly. 'He didn't get a single one.'

'Huh!' Dai sniffed disdainfully. 'What can you do with a stupid round thing like that? Rugby, now— that's what I call a game.'

'Soccer's much better!' protested Toby. 'Isn't it, Mum?'

Gina shook her head, laughing. 'No use expecting me to be referee. I know absolutely nothing about either of them—nor do I want to. I leave all that sort of nonsense to you men.'

Dai chuckled as he took her hands in his, pulling her to her feet beside him. 'I have my suspicions, Mrs B., that you know a good deal more about many things than you'd have us believe. Anyway, surely there's no such thing as a male province?' His arm fell naturally into place across her shoulders as they set off together along the path.

Her own arm creeping round his waist, she smiled up at him. 'If you say so. Where to now, Toby?'

Her son was in no doubt about that. 'To see the animals. I haven't seen the bears and elephants for ages. Did you know there's a way you can see them without going in the Zoo?' He trotted next to Dai, clutching his hand happily. 'You can look in through the fence and you can see the bears' place, and the elephants' house. Sometimes you can see them having a bath, and they squirt their keeper, and then he gives them their tea, and all the people are watching. Only they have to pay and you don't,' he explained kindly, in case Dai had missed the point.

'Is that right?' Dai grinned at him, and then raised a dark eyebrow at Gina. 'This boy should go far,' he observed. 'He's got his head screwed on.'

Gina's glance fell lovingly on Toby. 'Oh, I have every confidence he'll keep me in my old age.'

'I'd rather like to have a hand in that too,' remarked Dai quietly, as Toby ran on ahead to be first at the animals. When Gina didn't comment, he went on briskly, 'What's your opinion on Unification, Mrs Barton?'

'Unification?' For a second she halted in her tracks, bewildered by his apparent swing of mood.

'Fusion,' he elaborated patiently. 'The merging of lawyers' diverse roles into one. The abolition of separate duties for barristers and solicitors . . .'

'. . . bringing us into line with other western countries. Yes, I know what it means,' Gina asserted. 'I read the law journals too. I just didn't see what it had to do with . . . us, now.'

'So,' he pressed, 'have you any thoughts on the matter?'

They continued to stroll in perfect step. Gina kept her gaze fixed ahead to where Toby was heading energetically in the direction of his elephants. 'I've never thought it was a particularly good idea,' she said cautiously. 'After all, it seems to me we bring very different skills to the profession. I mean, barristers have to be extroverts, performers. Look how you rose to that Haines appeal—you could have won it standing on your head. Advocacy isn't my strong point. I made a real mess of it,' she recalled ruefully.

'But your briefings,' he muttered, 'are the finest I've ever encountered.'

Gina chose to ignore this cryptic interjection, suspecting it of not being in the best possible taste. 'No,' she continued thoughtfully, 'on balance I think we should stick to our own departments and make up an effective team, as we always have done.'

'But surely,' he pointed out airily, 'it was my sheer brilliance that got Peggy Haines off her charge. Not just any old Counsel could have done it—you hired one of the top men, don't forget, when you finally came to your senses.'

'And modest with it.' She wrinkled her nose at him. 'Well, Jim and Peggy were certainly bowled over by your achievement. You've got a pair of fans for life there. And even I have to admit you look rather stunning in the full regalia. I suspect you only joined the trade so that you could strut in the wig and gown.'

He hugged her against him and his deep laugh rumbled through her, seeming to emanate from within her own body. 'All right, I'll accept that we bring complementary assets to the partnership. If we didn't there wouldn't be a partnership.'

'Like males and females?' she suggested drily.

All at once he had stopped and was turning her to face him—drawing her closer. 'To sum up our own case, M'Lud, I contend that separate functions within a single operational unit must be the only possible course. Let's practise a spot of Fusion of our own, Gina.' Serious now, his eyes searched hers. His voice, low and intense, reached out to her senses. 'Two creatures—one flesh. Isn't that what we are?'

She nodded, her gaze riveted to his. Two creatures, one flesh. It was a true, an accurate description—and yet there was more, much more to it than that.

'I love you, Dai.' It was a calm, simple statement of fact. 'You know that.'

'I know it, Gina; and I could climb that Post Office Tower over there, and shout it out to the whole of London.' The man's face was split by a boy's grin. 'And I love you. And what's more, I'm in love with you. The two emotions are not necessarily inter-changeable.' Leaning down, he kissed her, lightly, on the mouth. Then his tone became urgent, persuasive. 'I need you Gina. I'll never be whole without you. Let's get married—as soon as your decree is made absolute. I know your experience of marriage has hardly been encouraging,' he went on, before she could find the words to respond, 'but after all, nor has mine. Here we both are—a pair of battle-scarred warriors. Are you going to be once bitten, twice shy—or shall we make a better job of it next time—together?' His hands gripped her upper arms—fierce, fervent. 'What do you think?'

Gina's gold-brown eyes stared up into his forceful

grey ones. In among the amazing joy and revelation of the last few weeks, this subject had threaded its way inevitably between them—always there, never quite mentioned. What *did* she think? Had the status of marriage been tainted, once and for all, by those youthful years—which now seemed far, far away in another, completely different world? Or was she prepared to try again—to take up the challenge Dai was offering her—to show them both that it could, after all, be successfully achieved?

Somewhere in the depths of her heart she had known the answer all along. Now it spilled out—a bubbling, uncontrollable certainty. 'I think, Dai,' she said slowly—and then smiled, 'I think that if you're prepared to take it on again, after what you went through—then so am I.'

His face lit up, but his eyes continued to search hers, questioning. 'You're absolutely sure, Gina? We can still be together, you know, on equal terms—whether we get married or not. In one way, it's only a formality . . .'

'No.' Her decision gathered momentum. 'I want to be married to you, Dai.' She reached up to take his face between her hands, bringing it down so that she could kiss him firmly on the lips. 'Married to you,' she said again, making quite certain he was left in no doubt, 'is what I want to be.'

He laughed aloud, and clasped her tightly to him. For a few seconds they stood, sharing a knowledge of complete understanding. Then Gina broke away to look up at him again. 'Just one thing, Dai. One thing to sort out.'

'And what might that be?' he demanded tenderly.

'Toby.'

The heavy brows arched enquiringly. 'Is there some problem about Toby?'

'Only that he exists. If you want me—it means taking him on as well. Whether he takes your name, or keeps Pete's—you'll be his father from now on.' Head

on one side, she regarded him quizzically. 'Sure it's
not too much for you?'

'Mrs Barton.' Dai expelled a long, weary sigh. 'For
a lady of exceptional intelligence you can be
remarkably obtuse. Haven't you guessed? It's Toby I
was really after all along. Surely you don't think I'd
have kicked up all this fuss about you in the first place
if it hadn't been for young Toby?' Breaking into an
irrepressible grin, he put his hands round her waist
and lifted her clear off the ground. 'Toby is an
inextricable part of the package. And preferably
several other little Tobys—all as much like you as it's
possible to be. Why?' He put her down, as the wicked
gleam momentarily faded. 'Don't you think he'll
approve of the idea?'

'He'll love the idea. He adores you already—you
know that. I was just . . .'

He laid a broad finger across her lips. 'There's no
more to be said, then, because the feeling is entirely
mutual. Now, where has the little devil got to?' He
turned, shading his eyes against the sun. Toby was a
blond, miniature blur—still exuding determination
even from a fair distance—up ahead. 'Let's go and tell
him he's about to become a two-parent family.'

'We'll have to catch him first,' Gina said; and they
ran hand in hand across the sunlit grass.

ATTRACTIVE, SPACE SAVING BOOK RACK

Display your most prized novels on this handsome and sturdy book rack. The hand-rubbed walnut finish will blend into your library decor with quiet elegance, providing a practical organizer for your favorite hard-or soft-covered books.

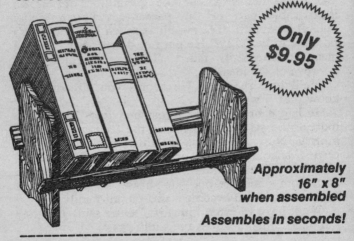

Only $9.95

Approximately 16" x 8" when assembled

Assembles in seconds!

To order, rush your name, address and zip code, along with a check or money order for $10.70* ($9.95 plus 75¢ postage and handling) payable to *Harlequin Reader Service*:

Harlequin Reader Service
Book Rack Offer
901 Fuhrmann Blvd.
P.O. Box 1325
Buffalo, NY 14269-1325

Offer not available in Canada.

BKR-1R

*New York residents add appropriate sales tax.

AT LAST YOU CAN FIND
TRUE ROMANCE ON TELEVISION!

PRESENTING THE SHOWTIME

Harlequin Romance Movie

S E R I E S

Full-scale romance movies, taken from your favorite Harlequin novels. Beautifully photographed on location, it's romance the way you've always dreamed. Exclusively on Showtime cable TV!

HARLEQUIN ON SHOWTIME
COMING ATTRACTIONS:

DREAMS LOST, DREAMS FOUND: Based on the novel by Pamela Wallace, starring Kathleen Quinlan.

ONLY ON SHOWTIME
This summer, you'll also see **Exclusive Movies** such as:
- **HEARTBURN** starring Meryl Streep, Jack Nicholson
- **RUTHLESS PEOPLE** starring Bette Midler
- **EXTREMITIES** starring Farrah Fawcett
- **KISS OF THE SPIDER WOMAN** starring William Hurt

HARLEQUIN ON SHOWTIME – THE ONLY
PLACE ON TV TO FIND TRUE ROMANCE!

SHOWTIME®

CALL YOUR CABLE COMPANY TODAY TO ORDER SHOWTIME

HMV-B-1

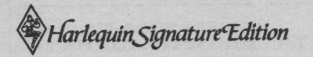

Harlequin Signature Edition

Carole Mortimer

Merlyn's Magic

She came to him from out of the storm and was drawn into his yearning arms—the tempestuous night held a magic all its own.

You've enjoyed Carole Mortimer's Harlequin Presents stories, and her previous bestseller, *Gypsy*.

Now, don't miss her latest, most exciting bestseller, *Merlyn's Magic*!

IN JULY

MERMG

All men wanted her,
but only one man would have her.

Her cruel father had intended
Angie to marry a sinister cattle baron twice her age.
No one expected that she would fall in love with his
handsome, pleasure-loving cowboy son.

Theirs was a love no desert storm would quench.

Available in JUNE or reserve your copy for May shipping by sending your name,
address, zip or postal code along with a check or money order for $4.70 (in-
cludes 75 cents postage and handling) payable to Worldwide Library to:

In the U.S.

Worldwide Library
901 Fuhrmann Blvd.
Box 1325
Buffalo, NY 14269-1325
Please specify title with book order.

In Canada

Worldwide Library
P.O. Box 609
Fort Erie, Ontario
L2A 5X3

 WORLDWIDE LIBRARY

STM-1

Take 4 best-selling love stories FREE
Plus get a FREE surprise gift!

Special Limited-Time Offer

Mail to   **Harlequin Reader Service®**

In the U.S.   In Canada
901 Fuhrmann Blvd.   P.O. Box 609
P.O. Box 1394   Fort Erie, Ontario
Buffalo, N.Y. 14240-1394   L2A 5X3

YES!   Please send me 4 free Harlequin Presents® novels
and my free surprise gift. Then send me 8 brand-new novels every
month as they come off the presses. Bill me at the low price of
$1.75 each*—a 10% saving off the retail price. There are no
shipping, handling or other hidden costs. There is no minimum
number of books I must purchase. I can always return a shipment
and cancel at any time. Even if I never buy another book from
Harlequin, the 4 free novels and the surprise gift are mine to keep
forever.   108 BPP BP7S

*$1.95 in Canada plus 89¢ postage and handling per shipment.

_____
Name   (PLEASE PRINT)

_____
Address   Apt. No.

_____
City   State/Prov.   Zip/Postal Code

This offer is limited to one order per household and not valid to present
subscribers. Price is subject to change.   HP-SUB-1A

In August
Harlequin celebrates

The **1000**th

Presents

Passionate Relationship

by
Penny Jordan

Harlequin Presents,
still and always the No. 1 romance
series in the world!

Available wherever paperback books are sold.

PR1000

Sarah

MAURA SEGER

Sarah wanted desperately to escape the clutches of her cruel father.
Philip needed a mother for his son, a mistress for his plantation.
It was a marriage of convenience.
Then it happened. The love they had tried to deny suddenly became a
blissful reality... only to be challenged by life's hardships and brutal
misfortunes.

Available in AUGUST or reserve your copy for July shipping by sending your name, address, zip or
postal code along with a check or money order for $4.70 (includes 75¢ for postage and handling) pay-
able to Worldwide Library to:

In the U.S.	In Canada
Worldwide Library	Worldwide Library
901 Fuhrmann Blvd.	P.O. Box 609
Box 1325	Fort Erie, Ontario
Buffalo, NY 14269-1325	L2A 5X3

Please specify book title with your order.

 **WORLDWIDE LIBRARY**

SAR-1